DEDICATION

To our faithful and loyal readers.
The voracious readers.
The vacation readers.
The bathroom readers.
We do this for you.
Enjoy!

RENEGADE

CASCADE MOUNTAIN MANHUNT

MIA LONDON
SUSAN SHEEHEY

Renegade
Cascade Mountain Manhunt Series
Book Two
by Mia London and Susan Sheehey

This is a work of fiction. Names, characters, places, and incidents either are the product of the author's imagination or are used fictitiously. Any resemblance to actual persons, living or dead, business establishments, events, or locales is entirely coincidental.

ISBN: 978-1947874183 (E-Book)
978-1947874206 (Paperback)

Publisher: Amepphire Press
11923 NE Sumner St, Ste 766015
Portland, OR 97220

Edited by Sharon Pickrel
Formatted by Leigh Stone
Cover design copyright © Romance Novel Covers Now

Published in the United States of America

RENEGADE
ROMANTIC SUSPENSE SERIES, BOOK 2

Librarian Lynée's perfect small-town life is overturned by an overbearing, bad-boy lawman on a motorcycle. His intentions are hardly friendly, and definitely not innocent.

Not with a vengeful cartel on his heels.

CHAPTER 1

FOR THE FIRST time in three months, Jace Ivy took a deep breath. With his gun on his hip, he sank into the bar stool at the Rock Road Diner, sipping hot coffee with his eye on the prize—Reed Monroe.

The vindicated joy racing through his veins was inexplicable. The same high as when he jumped out of a Cessna in Panama.

When he was given the assignment to bring in a rogue DEA agent suspected of shooting his partner, Jace was infuriated. No federal agent ever wanted to track and investigate one of their own. But after seeing the charges on this guy, he felt energized. Two other divisions had spent over half a year trying to find this guy with no results. Which is when they called him.

He couldn't wait to nail the guy's ass to the wall. He just had no idea it would take this flippin' long. Previous cases like this he'd solved within a few weeks. This one took over three months. And only because his target had goofed at a coffee shop with the security cameras, and his face hit their recognition software.

If Jace had a woman at home, she'd have divorced his ass by now.

Him married?

He chuckled out loud.

The waitress, Skye from her name tag, still looked stunned and frowned at his laughing.

"Sorry, sweetheart. Inside joke. How about I get my sandwich, then your cook there and me," he pointed with his fork, "can have a little chat?"

Skye nodded and scampered to the back to Monroe.

The small place was quaint, fall decorations dangling from the old ceiling tiles, and autumn wreaths hanging in the windows. Reminded him of a retro fifties diner complete with the red and white leathery plastic seats. Would've been cool if it were on purpose. But at least it was clean with the fresh lemon cleaner scent across the Formica counter. This place either stayed open only because it was the only place in this tiny town, or the food was that good. Hopefully, the latter.

He kept his gaze fixed on the chef, making sure he wouldn't run out the back door. The man had clearly been hiding out in this remote town east of the Cascade Mountains for a while. Long enough to establish a job and some connections, based on the intimate whisperings with this waitress.

A glance to his left and Jace noticed a strawberry blonde, her hair pulled back, glasses teetering on her nose, and lips like Tinkerbell. Her ultra-conservative clothes reminded him of an accountant or some kind of government worker. Like she was trying to blend into the dated scenery of the diner, only to fail miserably with that bright face.

"Morning." He felt like he should say something since she just stared at him with her mouth parted in shock. "In some cultures, it's considered rude to openly gawk at someone."

She blinked and straightened her back. "Sorry."

He couldn't be sure, but was she looking down her nose at him?

He chuckled again. Damn, this sleepy town could be a lot of fun. Too bad he wouldn't be around for long.

"Skye." The blonde waved to her friend, beckoning her.

The waitress returned and leaned in close to Tinkerbell.

"I should go, but I can stay if you need me."

Skye placed a hand over the blonde's. "No. I'm sure this is a misunderstanding. I'll call you later."

The blonde leaned in closer still. "Be careful."

Jace almost spat out his coffee, and some of it burned up into his nose. Several heads turned. He wiped his mouth to cover his smile.

Oh yeah. This assignment has definitely come to a glorious end.

Monroe came around the counter, pulling off his chef's apron. He let the thing dangle in his hand as he stopped several feet away. The look on his smoothly shaven face proved he knew exactly what Jace was here for.

He didn't look like he'd spent the last year on the run. He looked pretty damned happy where he was.

The whole diner had paused and watched the interaction like a thriller movie on a screen. Big audience. Which meant this guy was going to either make it super hard or as quiet as possible. There would be no middle ground. Given the amount of time it had taken to catch up to this guy, Jace almost wished Monroe would provide a little more drama at the end. Maybe give the blonde at the end of the counter a real show.

Jace took another sip of his coffee, then stood. The guy was a good four or five inches shorter, so it was easy to make himself look wider and in control. "Turn around. Hands on your head."

"Let me see your badge first." His voice was strangely calm.

With a smirk, he reached into his back pocket and pulled out his shiny DEA emblem in a black wallet. "Jace Ivy, Special Investigation Division. Satisfied?"

Monroe glanced at it. "This place closes in fifteen minutes. We have a lot to talk about. Perhaps you'd like to finish your food, then we can grab a booth."

Skye set the plate before him—club sandwich, chips, and a pickle spear. She nibbled her lower lip like it was coated with chocolate.

Jace nodded slowly. "All right." He lifted the top slice of bread off his club, investigating. "As long as you didn't put anything in here."

Monroe shook his head and grabbed a tomato slice from the top of the sandwich. Then popped it in his mouth. Proving at least the sandwich wasn't poisoned.

Jace frowned.

"Happy now?" the cook asked. "But, I'd watch her apple pie." His head jerked toward the waitress.

She gasped and smacked his upper arm.

"Give him a piece of pie on me, baby." Then he kissed the top of her head as he slipped on his apron to make the last orders for the hungry crowd.

Okay, so Reed found himself a woman to spend his time with. Interesting.

"Nuh-uh, Monroe. Out here with me."

Monroe turned. "I have a job to finish."

"So do I. You're not allowed out of my sight. I said you could have fifteen minutes until the place closes before I arrest you. I didn't say you could return back to the stoves where Lord knows how many knives you've got back there to use against me."

Monroe put his hands on his hips. "Then who will feed these customers?"

"I don't give a rat's ass. But it won't be you." He gestured to an empty booth. "Have a seat."

His suspect glared.

Damn, I love this part. He looked to the waitress. "I'd appreciate that slice of pie now."

The blonde Tinkerbell stood by the door, clutching a book to her chest and openly gawking at him.

He tossed her a wink.

CHAPTER 2

LYNÉE CLARK COULDN'T believe her eyes. Jace Ivy, Special Investigations Division. This scruffy, motorcycle-club-esque man was actually a lawman. Which didn't match anything in her mind of how an authority figure was supposed to look and act.

He was DEA, just like Reed. The rest of the town knew Reed Monroe as Guy Hancock, the newest addition to Cascade Creek. Her best friend's boyfriend, and a considerably better cook than Ralph, the diner's owner. True, Guy was an alias, which they'd learned over the last week. Guy was really an undercover agent on the run after being framed for murdering his former partner in El Paso. Or at least that's the story he told Skye. Which, of course, she then told her best friend, Lynée.

Lord, this Jace man was tall. When he gave her that wink, a whirlpool spiraled through her body, practically leaving her lightheaded. Now, he sat in a booth with his back to the wall opposite Reed, eating a piece of Skye's apple pie.

"Keep your hands on the table, where I can see them," he instructed Reed.

Walk away, Lynnie. But her feet just wouldn't move. She was completely mesmerized by this walking paradox. He was like a 12-car pileup—horrifying, disturbing, but she couldn't take her eyes away.

"Is there something I can help you with, honey?" the man asked, an all-too-confident smile on his lips. "You just can't stop staring. At least tell me your name."

Lynée frowned at his continued use of chauvinistic endearments. With a complete stranger. "Why? Am I under investigation, too?"

"Do you want to be?" His smile widened, stretching his lips to cut across his beard. He shoveled a piece of pie into his mouth.

"What's his charge?" she dared to ask. She had no idea where this bravery came from. As a librarian, she knew interfering with a police investigation was a criminal offense. But something compelled her to keep this guy talking.

"Lynée," Reed interrupted, "It's okay."

"Lynée?" Jace's gaze roved up and down her face, his fingers twirling the fork on the plate. "Beautiful name." His smile faded as he glanced back at Reed across from him. "He's charged with murder." The words hung in the air between them, and the whole diner quieted. "Among other charges. Killing your partner, a federal agent, is the most severe."

"I did *not* kill my partner," Reed replied calmly.

"You can tell me all about it back at the sheriff's office. Where we'll have our little fireside chat before I take you back to Seattle, and then have you transferred to El Paso." He pulled out his phone and started searching for a phone number.

"I strongly suggest you don't call them." Reed glanced at Skye, standing beside them.

"Why's that?" the man asked, almost bored.

"The cartel has a mole in the DEA."

Lynée held her breath. Expecting Jace to act surprised or at least pissed off. She actually didn't like her best friend standing so close to this bad boy with control issues.

He finished the last piece of pie and wiped his mouth with a napkin. "I know."

Reed blinked. "You do?"

"I'm looking at him."

CHAPTER 3

"*PUTA MADRE!*" CARLOS Cabello gripped the underside of his mahogany desk and flipped it, rage pulsing through every vein. Everything on the top scattered across the study, shattering the Virgin Mary figurine that had sat in the same spot for ten years.

The messenger, Tomas, cringed and moved back several feet. Carlos's second-in-command, Emilio, grabbed the man by the collar and yanked him back. He didn't acknowledge the porcelain shards skittering across his boots. The monstrous man knew not to react and not to allow the messenger to leave without being dismissed.

Carlos rarely became this emotional over anything. Except where that *damn boy* was concerned. His nephew, Diego Huerta, had always taken delight in dancing across his uncle's buttons. Now, despite all the cartel boss's efforts to keep that arrogant, impatient bastard safe, Diego was dead.

"I told that *pinche cabron* to go to the lake house, so I could clean up his mess." With a fiery rage in his eyes, he pulled the pistol from under his jacket, rushed over to Tomas, and jammed the barrel against his temple. The man shut his eyes and whimpered. "Why the hell didn't you *force* him to go? Throw him in the trunk and not let him out until you made it to Chalapa? How am I supposed to run my business against the DEA without Diego?"

"*No se, señor.*"

Carlos lowered his pistol but gripped the handle with white knuckles at his side. "Tell me precisely what happened."

Emilio let the man go and stepped back. Giving his superior the respect he deserved. He was an exceptional servant. Carlos wished he had a dozen more just like him. But now, he needed to interrogate the man who brought the news of the death of his nephew, the technical genius behind the cartel's digital era.

The messenger stammered his reply. "Huerta went to Seattle on his own, tracked the DEA agent to a motel. There was an altercation between them, and he was shot."

"The same DEA he's been on the hunt for all year?"

"*Si, señor.* Reed Monroe. He escaped. Along with a woman."

"What woman?"

"*No se.* The desk clerk said two people rented the room. A man and a woman. A blonde." He pulled out his phone and held up a picture. "I took this off the security camera footage. The police now have it."

Carlos took the phone and stared at the picture of that *bastardo* DEA agent, Reed Monroe. And some doe-eyed blonde woman, both standing outside the motel entrance. "Where is Diego's body?"

"In a Seattle morgue."

The cartel boss handed the phone back to Tomas and took a deep breath. The faint sound of the soccer game on the television in the corner helped calm him. He straightened his jacket, then holstered his pistol. "Get him. Bring his remains back here. I don't care how."

The man blinked. "All the way from Washington State? The body will—"

"Use a refrigerated truck! Do I have to think of everything? I will not allow my brother's son to be cremated and scattered in the United States. That mongrel country! Bring him home. Now!"

He waved his hand, dismissing the messenger. When he and Emilio were alone, Carlos motioned him closer to the windows. Overlooking the hills of northern Mexico, his hacienda was well hidden from any local spying. The balcony beyond the windows provided the perfect spot for a warm breeze on cool evenings like this one. But he couldn't chance anyone residing in the compound below hearing them. Though they were the family members of his henchmen—required to live within the compound walls— Carlos was still more careful than to allow prying ears.

"I'm sick of this chase," the cartel boss sighed. "My spy in the DEA hasn't been able to bring this man down either. All this money, for this *cucaracha* to keep slipping through my fingers." He cast his trusted friend a sideways glance. "Bring me this Monroe's head, with his dick shoved in his mouth. Put out a bounty. I want him dead before the DEA captures him. And if you're the one who finds him, I'll double the bounty."

His second-in-command nodded and turned to leave.

"Emilio?"

The man stopped.

"Both him and his *puta*. Make it painful."

CHAPTER 4

"KUDOS TO YOU for dodging our agents a whole year. Not an easy task." Jace studied his opponent, now in handcuffs across the table in the sheriff's interrogation room. It was small and stuffy, and as gray as a Seattle sky.

Monroe scoffed. "Dodging the cartel was harder."

"I bet. You had some pretty nasty bastards after you." Jace held up a few black and white photos of dead men's faces, covered in blood. "These two cartel thugs were found dumped in a river outside Wenatchee. And you just happen to be holed up in a tiny town a short distance away. Coincidence?"

Monroe never lifted his eyes from the table. According to Sheriff Wyatt, the suspect was just as silent the entire ride over to the county office. Didn't make a single sound, nor seemed the least bit nervous.

Jace leaned forward. "Looks like your murder tally just got upped to three." He stood and slowly walked around the table. With a single finger, he pulled down the high neck of Reed's sweater. Revealing nasty bruises all the way around. "Where'd you earn that horse collar?"

"I tripped." Monroe cast scornful eyes at him.

"Into someone's vicious grip? Or while you were dumping the bodies? Come on. You've been in and out of

Seattle a half a dozen times this past month. That's how those guys tracked you. Hell, that's how I tracked you. I have your face recorded in a nearby coffee shop. Just sitting there glued to your laptop for hours."

Monroe chuckled and shook his head. But he stayed silent.

"Pathetic disguise you wore, by the way. Fake glasses and a ball cap? Got your truck's license plates off the bank's security footage from across the street of the coffee shop. Made it all too easy to follow you here through traffic cameras."

The man still wouldn't talk. Normally throwing additional evidence on top of suspects' heads, they'd cave under the weight. The threat of an even worse sentence. They'd always give something. But not this one. He was either really fucking stupid or trained very well.

"You were driving hours out of your way to hack into servers, hiding your footprints by piggy-backing off someone else's WiFi signal. Must've been really important. Did you have fun?"

"Do you think I haven't been through this before? Interrogated with the tough guy routine?"

Jace sighed. "I know you have. Where you somehow escaped your handcuffs and strolled right out of the El Paso division like you owned it."

"Not bad for a tech geek, huh?"

Smug sonuvabitch.

Jace leaned his hands menacingly on the table. "They underestimated you. A mistake I won't make. I've read your entire file. I know how you earned a living prior to the DEA. By the time we're through, you won't touch another computer or smartphone for the rest of your life."

Monroe shook his head. "Then why tell you anything?

No matter what I do, you'll string me out to dry."

Jace sat down and leaned his elbows on the table. "I'll keep the cartel off your ass. We'll have a nice, cuddly cell waiting for you along with three meals a day and Big Bang Theory reruns on the community TV. It's the least you deserve for killing your partner. Cabello, on the other hand, will have a special torture chamber set up for you and keep you alive God knows how long to inflict as much pain as any human *can't* take."

For some reason, Monroe didn't seem scared or even anxious at that little detail. With a lazy expression, he finally looked up at Jace. "Cabello knows everything you know. He has access to all of it. I have the evidence to prove it. Someone in the DEA is tipping him off. My partner discovered it and was in the process of finding out who it was. They killed him for it, and came after me."

Jace leaned back in his chair, the creak echoing off the walls. Finally, he was talking. "Which is when you turned yourself in to the El Paso office. *Two days later.* Enough time to wipe all your evidence off the hard drives you turned in."

Reed's mouth parted.

That one struck home. Jace tried hard not to smile. "Didn't think I knew that detail, did you?"

"When I turned those in, those backup drives were full. Are you saying they're empty?"

"Don't act surprised, Monroe. You already knew that."

His jaw tensed. "It's all wrapped up in one, pretty fucking bow for them. Why else would the DEA have to dig any further?" he mumbled to himself. Then he buried his forehead in his cuffed hands.

Jace pulled out his phone and started to call for a transfer. After all, he was only brought onto this case to find and capture Monroe. He'd leave the official investigation into this guy's crimes for the El Paso folks. Another case solved. He could finally go back home.

"If I was guilty," the suspect continued, "why would I have turned myself in? If I had wiped everything, I could've just walked away and disappeared for good. You'd've had nothing to chase."

He paused before he hit the call button.

Monroe's gaze turned hard. "I thought it was a damn debriefing," he snapped. "I followed protocol for undercover agents. The first step is to lose any tails, then come in. *With* all evidence. There's a confirmed mole in the DEA. Clearly capable of deleting reports from our own systems. From wiping hard drives *after* they've been turned in. You're not a techie, Ivy, but you're not a dumbass either. They're getting rid of everyone and everything associated with the Cabello investigation. I'm the last one. You yourself said they were after me. Then how could I be the mole?"

Jace stared at the man for a long time. For a former identity-thief like Monroe, disappearing would've been easy for him. Hell, he'd accomplished that much for a full year. Why would Monroe continue to research the psycho cartel boss after he'd successfully disappeared?

"Shit," he whispered. Then he put his phone back in his pocket. Dammit, he just wanted a clean-cut, get-in-get-out case. His gut yelled that something wasn't right. As tight-lipped as this suspect was, he had a point. Maybe he didn't kill his partner. Just maybe, this was all a cover-up. "You said you had the evidence to prove Cabello is working with a mole?"

Monroe clasped his cuffed hands together on the table. "You believe me?"

"Not yet. But show me that evidence, and I'll do

21

everything I can to help you."

He shook his head. "How do I know I can trust you? You could be the mole."

He cast his gaze to the ceiling. "We don't have time for this."

A chime on his phone made Jace pull it from his pocket. His boss sent him a text.

Cabello issued contract on Reed Monroe for nephew's murder. Cartel hitmen en route. Find him and bring him in ASAP.

"Fuck."

"What?" Monroe asked.

"Your time is up. Is your alleged evidence close by?"

"Why?"

"Because the Cabello cartel has just issued a contract on your head for killing one of their own. Assassins are coming for you. I have to get you out of here now."

His eyes widened. In three seconds, his whole face paled. "I can't leave without Skye. They'll find her."

"Why? Was she there when you killed these guys? Which one's the nephew?"

He pursed his lips and glanced around the room.

"I'm your only chance right now. You have to turn over what you have."

"Put Skye in protective custody, and I'll give you everything."

CHAPTER 5

JACE LISTENED THROUGH the three rings.

I need insight on this one. I'll go to the one person I can trust to guide me.

"Hey, slugger, how are you?" Philip Sterling, his mentor and father's best friend, answered the phone as his usual cheerful self. "How's your golf game?

Jace chuckled out loud. "No time for golf these days."

"Right, so how's your assignment going? Still chasing after that undercover delinquent?" Phil asked. His scraggly voice sounded a little distracted, but at least he had the time to answer Jace's call.

He scraped his hand along the back of his neck. "Yeah, but it's complicated. That's why I'm calling."

"You?" He snorted. "You could write a book on complicated."

"Yeah, real page-turner. Look, I caught up with him."

The line went quiet.

"Phil?"

"Took you long enough," he laughed. "Congrats, Jace. Another case in the bag. I'm sure you've earned some well-deserved time-off after this one."

"That's just it. I'm not sure I can hand him over yet."

"What do you mean?"

Jace took several steps away from the interrogation room door and moved toward the lobby. "What has the El Paso division done about this mole? I can't ask them this question if the cartel rat is, in fact, out of that office. If I transfer him back, we'll be turning over the only witness to corroborate his partner's reports on the cartel."

There was a rustling on the other end. From the clear voice on the other end, Phil just took him off speakerphone. "You don't think he's the mole?"

"I'm not sure. I'd rather make the mistake of believing him than putting an innocent agent in prison." Jace looked up. Through the front office windows, he spotted the Tinkerbell blonde from the diner sitting on the lobby benches. Lynée. She sat next to her waitress friend, Skye. Who chewed on her finger like a neurotic on ten cups of coffee. Hell, had they been sitting out there this whole time?

"Have you told any of your superiors this?" his mentor asked over the phone.

"Not yet. Look, I know fieldwork is beneath you now that you're all cooped up in your fancy office at headquarters..."

"Kiss my ass. Your father woulda smacked you for that comment."

He forced himself to look away from Lynée, her adorable face too distracting. "I'm only asking if you were staring down the barrel of this case, what would you do?"

After a heavy sigh, his mentor continued. "Well, it's not my area anymore. But first, I would secure any evidence he has." The unmistakable sound of an opening soda can clearly showed Phil hadn't kicked his caffeine habit. "If he really isn't the mole, it's his only thing to prove it. Second, I'd stash him somewhere safe the DEA doesn't know about. But let me ask you one important question. Is this guy worth risking your career? Because if you're wrong, and he's really the mole, you'll be lucky if you don't end up with charges yourself."

Jace swallowed hard. "If you were being framed for something, wouldn't you want someone to give you a chance to prove it? If all the evidence together, combined with what he gives me, isn't enough to exonerate him, I'll drag him into that trial room myself. Fully shackled and muzzled. But if it proves he's telling the truth, I'd be handing him over to slaughter. And the cartel gets to keep their rat. You know I can't stand for that."

A low growl on the other end proved his point. "Fuckin' rats. The El Paso division has always been the most susceptible. Shows the cartel can get to anyone. So you have to keep this guy under lock and key. Tell your boss where you are in case those thugs catch up with you. But don't tell anyone else. Not even me."

Jace couldn't help another glance at Lynée, holding her friend's hand. The nonchalant way she pushed her black-rimmed glasses up her nose was completely irresistible. Laying in her lap sat a manila envelope.

"You hear me?" Phil urged.

"Yeah, got it. By the way, that soda you're drinking better not have any sugar."

"It's diet, jackass. What are you, my wife? Go fix your own fucking business."

The line clicked dead. Jace chuckled. He really knew how to pulverize that man's last nerve. Hell, he's been fraying them since he was a kid. He followed in the same footsteps as his father, much to Phil's regret.

He stuck his phone back in his pocket.

CHAPTER 6

"THEY CAN'T DO this to him," Skye whispered in the lobby. "Reed is innocent."

"It'll be okay," Lynée urged, patting her friend's hand. With a quick glance at the clock, it had been four hours since they took Reed away in the back of the sheriff's squad car. The federal agent had followed on his motorcycle and Skye behind them in her car. Lynée had immediately gone to the library to do a quick search and then met up with her best friend to keep her company. The sheriff's office was next door, so it was easy to skip out of work early.

She imagined a lot of these interrogations could be twice as long as this, but she knew her best friend wouldn't leave. Not without seeing Reed again.

"Wyatt, how much longer?" Skye asked the sheriff.

The balding man with white scruff on his chin looked up from his desk on the other side of the lobby window, sitting open.

"This is a DEA investigation. I don't call the plays. You probably should head home."

"Fat chance of that," Lynée scoffed.

The bearded federal agent appeared from behind the lobby window, talking on the phone. From his furrowed brow and scrunched up shoulders, he was irritated. Maybe things weren't going well in the interview room. Whatever was going on, Lynée was certain she didn't want to be in the chair opposite that man. Intimidating as heck. Easily over six-feet with a perfect, brooding disposition, Jace Ivy sent all her mental red alarms into overdrive. Including the dormant hot buttons she hadn't used since her marriage. They were all screaming too.

Skye had urged her to start dating again after the fiasco with Todd, her ex-husband. Lynée had successfully dodged each attempt her friend had tried to set her up with. No way in hell would she start with this guy. Despite his compliments and roving stare at the diner.

He looked over at them and ended his call. Somehow his features turned even more serious. Lynée hadn't thought that was possible.

Her heart hammered against her sternum. What was that mountain of muscles thinking?

Probably some Wild West cliché of a lawman always gets his man.

He disappeared behind the walls of the lobby. Walls that held big secrets that only badges got to know. Or criminals. He reemerged through the reinforced doors many long minutes later, the metal clicking noise of the lock echoing throughout the empty lobby.

"Skye Winters?" His voice almost boomed in Lynée's ears.

Skye shot to her feet. "Where's Reed?"

"Come with me." He was so gruff and unpleasant.

Lynée frowned. They had done nothing to deserve this kind of treatment. Everyone was cooperating, and this pistol of a man had apparently not learned that one catches more bees with honey than vinegar.

Skye's hand tightened in hers. Her whole face had gone

pale. Which ticked Lynée off even more.

"If you're going to question her, she should probably have an attorney with her." She lifted her chin, forcing herself to have more confidence than she felt.

Jace's gaze slowly moved up and down Lynée, something flickering in his eyes as he did.

Shit. I've pissed off the brooding lawman.

Her mouth turned dry, but there was no way she would back down. This was her best friend he was threatening.

"This is not a questioning. Miss Winters is not in trouble. But I need to speak to her. Alone."

"The hell you are," Skye shot back. "She's coming with me. I need to see Reed."

"You don't dictate the terms. I'm doing Reed a favor here. Both of you are in danger. Your best move is to shut up and follow instructions."

Lynée blinked. "Danger?"

Skye cast a stunned glance her way, and her clammy hand tightened around Lynée's.

Despite the rudeness of the man's statement and tone, maybe following his directions was in their best interests. At least while Reed was in custody. Lynée nodded with a reassuring smile to her friend and released her hand.

Skye followed him, her chin held high.

"Excuse me, Mr. Ivy?" Lynée stepped forward.

Both he and Skye stopped in the doorway. His expression changed to one of curiosity. Even amusement.

"First of all," she cleared her throat, "you need to work on your manners when addressing a woman."

His eyebrows nearly hit his shaggy hairline.

"Secondly," she shoved the envelope out, the edge hitting his broad chest, "this is a list of all the federal agents in the last ten years who were falsely accused and later exonerated on charges of working for the cartel. The conviction rate is less than ten percent."

He glanced at the envelope like it was an insult. "How did you get this information?"

"I'm a librarian. Research is what I do best."

Very slowly, the corner of his mouth tilted up. Cracking the rough, intimidating facade just enough to warm her cheeks.

"Surely, research can't be the *only* thing you're good at. Miss...?"

"Clark." Her cheeks nearly burned. Just what exactly was he implying?

"Do you really want to help your friends, Lynée?" The question came out softer, his tone almost caressing her nerves in ways she didn't dare admit she liked. Because fudge, the way his eyes sparkled like that—like he was setting a trap for her just because he could—she might as well be a deer drawn to a sugar lick.

"Of course," she whispered, suddenly out of breath. Then with more conviction because she meant it. "Of course. I'll help her any way I can."

His grin widened. "Let me borrow your car."

***

Jace hated having to leave his motorcycle in the sheriff's department's car lot. Still, at least it was gated, and he had a fabric cover for it in his lockbox on the back of the bike. Sure, his prized possession wasn't that practical on the job, completely incapable of transporting a suspect, but it gave him confidence. He'd be back for it by tomorrow, God willing. But he couldn't use it for the next task. At least the sheriff had been a decent guy and let him store it there, free of charge.

He patted the handlebars over the cover. "Be good. Play nice with the other bikes. I'll be back soon."

A brisk breeze blew in his face, swirling the dead leaves in the lot up and around him. An incoming rainstorm wasn't far off. He pulled his leather jacket higher up on his neck. He turned to the trio behind him, waiting beside Lynée's Honda Civic. He held out his hand for the keys.

Lynée shook her head. "I said you could use it. Not drive it. Just tell me where we're going." Those big, blue eyes and pouty, pink Tinkerbell lips glared up at him.

He scowled. "You can't know where they're going. That's the point."

The blonde scoffed in a way that made him want to shake that look off her face. Or perhaps kiss it off. She looked like she could use a good one. "Like I'm going to tell anyone where they'll be. They mean more to me than to you." She opened the driver's door and climbed in, shooting him a defiant look. "Get in."

Skye looked at him apprehensively. She hadn't stopped gripping Monroe's hand since they left the interview room. Where he'd reluctantly uncuffed him and swore that if he tried to run, Jace would plug a few bullets into the guy's back.

"Is she always this stubborn?" he asked the waitress.

Lynée chuckled. "Hello, Mr. Pot. So judgmental of us kettles." She climbed into the back seat. Monroe followed her without giving him a second look.

Jace took the front seat and actually had to sink into the seat. The tiny car barely fit his six-foot-three frame. He swore his motorcycle sat higher off the ground than this thing. He shifted and twisted in the seat, trying to get comfortable. Almost immediately regretting asking to use her car. Sure, he could've asked the sheriff to borrow a police vehicle to transport his witnesses, but that would draw too much attention. He needed an unmarked car, just in case someone had this guy followed.

"Where to?" Lynée asked, starting up the heater.

"To get Monroe's evidence. Then to a safe house near Seattle. It's a great place for them to hide out in," Jace answered, glancing in the back seat to be sure Monroe couldn't jump out that easily. "Monroe, I need you to sit on the other side."

His suspect sighed. "Seriously? If I wanted to run, I would've done that already."

"Where I can see you. Now."

He gave Skye an apologetic look, knowing she would be stuck sitting behind Jace where he'd backed up the seat as far as it would go.

"That's a horrible idea." Lynée cast him a sideways glance. She pulled onto the main drive.

"The suspect must always sit where I can see his hands. He's lucky I don't have his ass cuffed."

"No, I meant a DEA safe house. That place is obviously in the records somewhere. If there's a mole in your agency, you want to take them somewhere none of your colleagues know about."

Jace gaped at the beautiful blonde in horror. "How the hell does she know about this?" He glared at Monroe. "You don't give a damn about confidentiality, do you? That'll be another thing they want to throw the book at you for."

Monroe chuckled. "With the other charges they want to hang me on, you think I'm shaking in my boots about confidentiality?"

"I told her," Skye chimed in.

"Easy on the language, please," Lynée cut in. "And lighten up, Agent Ivy." She pulled out of the parking lot, adjusting her seatbelt to rest between her breasts more comfortably. Giving him a clue just how deep the crevice between those delectable mounds was.

Dammit, he shouldn't be focusing on that. "It's *Special* Agent Ivy."

"Well, I'm not calling you that. You already have a pompous enough attitude. How about Jace?"

"Who are you calling pompous, Miss I-Won't-Let-Anyone-Drive-My-Car?" Holy hell, she was infuriating. "And where the hell is your computer equipment, Monroe?"

Skye looked at her boyfriend, and when he nodded, she answered for him. "At my house."

The whole car was silent for the drive over to Skye's house, which was the way Jace liked it. Every time that Tinkerbell woman opened her mouth, she started to rattle him.

They pulled up to a small home with two large windows flanking a wooden door and a mature birch tree in the front lawn. They all climbed out, and he stopped them on the front porch. "Turn around," he instructed Monroe. Then pulled out his handcuffs.

"Are you serious?" he shot back.

"You're not allowed to touch anything. I don't want you trying to pull a weapon on me in there, or worse, destroy evidence."

"You are so paranoid," Skye muttered under her breath.

Jace gave her a hard look. "I have another set of cuffs for you if you don't watch it, so don't test me."

She scowled at him and opened her front door. "All the boxes are in my bedroom closet."

The place was neat, kinda whimsical with a mix of antique and modern furniture and rugs. Seemed to suit her.

"You stay with me, Monroe." He gently nudged him forward as they moved to the back bedroom. He glanced into every open door on the way down, making sure they were alone. If the cartel really was after this guy, he couldn't be too cautious in thinking they couldn't track them back to the girlfriend's house.

When he was sure there weren't intruders, he made Monroe sit on the bed. "I want you two ladies to stay where I can see you at all times. You're not allowed to touch anything."

Skye rolled her eyes and opened her closet. Four full bags and a few boxes sat on the floor. "This is everything we had."

With a quick glance behind him to make sure Monroe still sat on the bed, he opened each bag. Mostly computer equipment, some weapons and ammunition, and a change of clothes. "Where are your thumb drives?"

"Spread throughout the bags," he answered. "And then two more in the kitchen junk drawer."

Skye sat beside him, her hand clasped to his, and kissed his cheek.

The lovey-dovey shit was starting to get on Jace's nerves.

"I don't have time to search the whole place right now." He zipped everything up and stood. "I'll come back for a further sweep after I get you settled. But if there's anything else hidden, either here or anywhere else, you have to tell me. It's the only way I can help you."

"This is it. These bags and the drives in the kitchen."

"Are you sure? Where have you been staying all these weeks? Anything left there?"

Reed scratched at the collar of his shirt. "I cleaned out the cabin I was staying in after I was attacked. Courtesy of those two cartel thugs whose post-mortem pictures you were kind enough to show me. I don't think I left anything behind other than some clothes and my security cameras."

"Where's the footage from the cameras?"

"On the drives in the bags."

Lynée hugged herself in front of the windows, clearly uncomfortable. But the light streaming between the blinds framed her strawberry blonde head in such an angelic way and brought to mind other heavenly visions.

Snap out of it, man.

"If I find anything hidden somewhere else, including at that cabin, I'll drag you out of the safehouse and beat you to a pulp myself." He held out his hand to Skye. "Give me your phone."

She eyed him. "Why?"

"You can't take it with you. In case they're tracking you too. You wouldn't want to lead these crazy suckers right to the front door, would you?"

She huffed, dug out her phone, and handed it over.

He set it on the dresser. Then led them back out to the car and loaded the evidence in the trunk. He directed Lynée toward the highway, but she headed north instead of west. "What are you doing?"

"I told you. A DEA safe house is a stupid idea. There's another place they can go, and it's closer."

"You are not going to hijack my suspect or my case, Miss Clark. Do as I say."

"And you're not going to put my best friend and her boyfriend in danger." She sighed. "Listen, is it about getting your way or about keeping them safe?"

"Safety. Of course."

"Then do you think you can take some input from a woman? For once?"

He shifted in his seat to face her. *Seriously?* "I have no problem taking direction from women, Miss Clark. But perhaps you failed—"

"Good. Then I know a place." She shot a wink at her friend through the rearview mirror. "We might need to stop for some supplies too since they won't have transportation. Don't you agree, *Special* Agent?"

Oh, this little five-foot-five dynamo was now buttering him up as she mocked him. He shook his head in the total exasperation with it all. What had he trampled in to?

If there wasn't an audience, he'd yank the wheel, have her pull over, and take her across his knee this very moment. She may not enjoy it, but he *definitely* would.

CHAPTER 7

AN AWKWARD, HOUR-LONG drive ended in pulling up to a small cottage snuggled in an alcove at Lake Chelan. Several back roads twisted and turned around the mountain until it dropped them into this fairly remote section of the lake.

Jace watched their tail, happy not to see a damn car behind them for the last twenty miles.

The deep cerulean blue of the lake shimmering off the autumn sunlight through the clouds surprised Jace. He expected lakes up in these mountains to be darker, muddier, and certainly not this clear—particularly late in the year. If he didn't know any better, he might've assumed they were in the middle of an Ozarks summer.

The second they stepped outside, the cold temperatures slapped him in the face, bringing him back to reality.

"My parents are in Florida for the winter, so you can use it for however long you need." Lynée smiled at her friend as she pulled out one of their bags.

"There's a storm coming in later," Skye announced. "We should get things settled before then. We also need some groceries."

"First thing's first." Jace followed Lynée up the small

porch steps and waited for her to enter. He let Monroe and Skye follow, and asked them all to sit on the couch while he grabbed a trash bag from the kitchen pantry. Then he moved from room to room, removing every telephone, wireless router, and antenna he found. He collected them all into the bag and carried it back to the entryway.

"What are you doing?" Skye asked, wrinkles marring her forehead.

"Absolutely no electronics allowed." He dropped the bag by the door, then fished around the kitchen for anything else Monroe could use to contact someone or get online.

"You are so paranoid," Skye groaned.

He ignored her criticisms and pulled out a burner phone from his back pocket. He set it on the kitchen table.

"No one has this number but me. It won't allow you to make any calls except for my phone. If it rings, you answer. Day or night." He moved to the family room where the lovebirds crowded together on the small sofa, and Lynée sat on the antique rocking chair in the corner. He sat on the coffee table, the sturdy reclaimed wood creaking. He rested his elbows on his knees, giving them his authoritative tone for this next bit. "You are not allowed to leave these walls for any reason. If there's an emergency, you call me. Prowler outside, you cut your thumb off with a steak knife, or your appendix bursts...you don't call the paramedics. You call me."

"But you're more than an hour away. What if—" Skye started.

He cut her off. "You. Call. Me."

"What if we run out of toilet paper?" Monroe's smug smile just begged to be punched.

"Use your goddamn hand for all I care." He stared hard at Monroe. "You are *not*, under any circumstances, allowed to touch a computer, smartphone, or anything that allows you access to the Internet. Hell, for the time being, the fucking toaster is off-limits. Just that phone." He pointed to the burner on the table.

Monroe smirked. "How about a flashlight?"

The table creaked again as Jace leaned forward. "Not even that. If it has a battery or plugs into an outlet, the answer is no." He moved his gaze to Skye. "If you care about him and want him to survive this, you need to make sure he follows these rules. Leaving the two of you here alone without supervision relies heavily on the honor system. If you break the rules, these monsters will find you. If they don't, then you'll at the very least face obstruction charges from me."

Skye swallowed but stared hard back at him. "Message received. You can back down a skosh, Kujo."

He stood and clapped his hands together. This next part was going to be fun. "Now, if I could request the ladies to please get whatever essentials you'll need from the grocery store, I need to ask *Reed* here a few questions." He pulled out his wallet and handed Lynée a few hundred dollars in cash.

When she grabbed the bills, his fingers didn't let go right away. He waited for her curious gaze to meet his. She scowled at his playful gesture, and he couldn't help but smile.

Skye fidgeted on the couch, her grip tightening on Monroe's hand. "What are you going to do?"

"Not to worry." Jace smiled. "If he behaves, I'll behave."

***

Jace pinched the bridge of his nose. "You're saying the

cartel coordinated their multi-million dollar operation through a video game?"

Monroe scraped his hand through his tousled hair. "An online gaming app. Dark Inferno. They used the in-game chat function to communicate drop shipments and times. Even accepted payments through their system. Joe somehow stumbled onto them using it and initiated most of his contacts that way."

"Why didn't he tell you about it?"

He huffed, and his whole face turned hard. "At the time, he thought I was the mole."

"Why would he think that?"

"I've been asking myself that question for a whole damn year. Maybe because I used to be a gamer, too. He never said why in his reports."

Jace leaned back in his chair, trying to stretch his back muscles. They'd been sitting in the same spot for nearly an hour as he questioned him. The women were still at the store, thank goodness. He was certain Monroe wouldn't be nearly as cooperative if his girlfriend hung over his shoulder the whole time.

"That's another thing. I don't have reports from him going back to more than a month before his death. You said you saw him writing out his reports every week. Where are those files?"

On a long sigh, Monroe flattened his hands on his lap. "Joe kept a separate file with his notes, offline from DEA systems, and logged every time he submitted his reports. In that file, he noted that around the beginning of October, his reports were missing. Which is right around the time he moved out of our safe house. And subsequently stopped communicating with me."

"Did he think you were the one deleting them?"

Monroe shrugged. "Maybe. But it wasn't me. I didn't hear from him again until the night he died."

"Where did Joe keep this separate file?"

"On a personal cloud drive. Wasn't easy to get into, either."

Jace cringed. This was getting more convoluted. "We'll come back to that in a minute. Tell me more about this game. The one who designed it works for the cartel?"

"Diego Huerta. Also goes by Daniel, and his username was LocoLobo."

"Crazy wolf." Jace snorted. Was he one of the dead guys in the morgue from Wenatchee? Was he one of the ones who'd been sent to kill Monroe?

"He used one of the shell companies to create this game and used it to coordinate drug distribution. He's the one who killed Joe in the warehouse."

"Whoa. Back up. How did he go from app developer to gun-toting cartel hitman?"

Monroe threw up his hands. "How did I go from a black hat cybercriminal to an undercover DEA agent? We're not all geeky, pale-faced introverts surviving on hot pockets and techno music. This isn't the nineties. Would you drop the clichéd stereotype?"

"Fine." Jace scrubbed at his chin, the beard turning itchy. "How did you find out about him?"

"I followed the name. That's what I was researching for hours in the Seattle coffee shop. Along with every other username in Joe's chat sessions. Dug into anyone with a technology background. When I found Huerta, his picture came up, and I recognized him. He's somehow related to the Cabello family."

Jace bit on his tongue. Based on the text from his superior, he guessed this Huerta guy was Carlos Cabello's nephew. The fact that Monroe didn't know that meant the cartel had clearly hidden that biological relationship for a reason. "Where is this Huerta guy now?" He already knew the answer, but he had to test Monroe and make sure he was telling the truth.

His witness dropped his gaze to the table. It was a long few seconds before he finally answered. "Dead."

Jace raised an eyebrow. "How?"

He pushed up from the couch and crossed the room to stare out the window. "He caught up with Skye and me in Seattle. In a motel."

"You mean, he tracked you. From all the research you'd done on the game?"

He shrugged. "Probably. He was as good a techie as me."

Jace humphed and studied the gray-beige tile on the kitchen floor. "Everyone can be gotten to. One way or another. You're lucky you made it out alive."

He turned, arms crossed. "I never want to put Skye in that position again." The severity in his eyes proved easily enough how much he loved the woman.

"Well, hopefully, that's something I can help you with. As long as you've told me everything you know. All your research is on those hard drives?"

Monroe nodded. "All of it."

"Okay. I'm trusting you on this. As I go through your evidence, if I have questions, I'm going to call on that phone. If there's any malware on those drives, tell me now."

Crunching gravel outside drew their attention to the window. Lynée and Skye returned from the grocery store, and the trunk popped open.

The pair of them stood to go help unload. Jace stopped him. "I'll help them. You write down every single username and password on those drives. Also, give me the address to that cabin."

Jace scooped the bags out of Lynée's hands. "I've got these."

Her eyes went wide, and a flush crept across her cheeks. "'Kay. Thanks."

In the kitchen, the three of them unpacked and put everything away. By the number of bags, they should have enough food to last them for a couple weeks. Jace also noticed they also hadn't returned with any change, either.

Figures.

Skye pulled a box from one of the bags and waved it for her boyfriend to see. "I thought you'd like these, Reed."

Jace spotted the jumbo box of hot pockets.

He nearly burst out laughing.

Monroe shot him a death look. "Shut up."

CHAPTER 8

THE BROODY, RUDE special agent was silent for the first half of the drive back to Cascade Creek. Which Lynée was grateful for since her patience for his rough-handed, cocky attitude was wearing out. He spent the whole time checking the side mirror and studying the mountainside.

Twilight crept between the hills, and light rain started on the other side of the pass. She flipped on the windshield wipers, along with the defroster. She wasn't that cold with her oversized sweater, though the oversized, sack of muscles beside her did more than a well enough job heating up the car.

A thousand questions swirled in her mind. But if she opened her mouth to ask any of them, that meant listening to his sarcasm and condescending response. That is *if* he answered any of her questions. He seemed determined to keep everyone in the dark as much as possible. Which Lynée deduced was more power-hungry than safety-focused.

The headlights flashed against the bright green sign displaying Cascade Creek only five miles away. She couldn't bear to wait any longer. "How long do you think it will take to solve this?"

"Why?" he asked gruffly without looking at her.

"I don't want them to be stuck up there any longer than

required. How long will your job take?"

"I've already finished my job."

Lynée stared at him, the car veering a bit too close to the edge of the road, where the cliff dropped off a good hundred feet. She swerved back into her lane.

"Eyes on the road, Tinkerbell." He finally looked at her. "Do you want me to drive?"

It took her several seconds to calm her heart rate. "No." She didn't even know where to start, the offensive nickname he'd just coined for her or his first statement. "What do you mean you already finished?"

"My orders were to find and arrest Reed Monroe. I did that."

"Then what are we doing now?"

"We? Nothing. I'm following a lead on a different crime. You're driving me back, and that's where your involvement ends." He kept his serious gaze on hers, a little too intensive for her tastes.

"Not a chance, bub. And don't call me Tinkerbell."

From the side of her eyes, she spotted the edge of his mouth lift.

Good Lord, she needed to keep her attention on the road.

"Did Reed or Skye give you anything to hold for them? Or hide?"

She blinked. Where did that come from? "Of course not."

"You sure? Your best friend you've known your whole life didn't trust you to hold something for her, just in case she needed it later?"

"Like what?"

He turned his body to face her a little more. "You tell me. Because if you don't, it's obstruction of justice. People do time for that."

Lynée huffed. Wow, this guy was a piece of work. Her knuckles turned white on the steering wheel. "Do you insult every person whom you ask for a favor or just the ones in this town? Skye is not a criminal. If she had something or gave something to me to hold, she would've told you about it herself. She doesn't have a dishonest bone in her body. Nor do I. Your assumption otherwise is offensive."

He started to chuckle. Like he'd been staring at something amusing or something worth mocking. "My assumptions over the years have rarely been wrong. You'd be stunned at the things I've seen when someone wants to escape the law. Including hiding things for best friends. Sometimes in very...interesting places."

She felt her eyes nearly bug out of their sockets at that comment. The man's smile only widened from the passenger seat, infuriating her further.

Stop reacting, Lynée. He's only saying these things to get a rise out of you.

She forced herself to calm down, and instead focused on the road and pretending that nothing more than a sack of rotten groceries sat beside her.

"You are so cute when you seethe."

Lynée adjusted the rearview mirror. Anything to keep her hands from strangling him. She didn't have any violent tendencies in her personality, but the urge to slap him itched in her fingers. Being around this man had tilted her whole world sideways in less than a day, and then he had the audacity to heckle her.

Skye and Reed needed her help. She needed to stay close to whatever Jace Ivy was going to uncover so she could get her best friend back. After all, she was the one who'd urged Skye to help Reed in the first place. Her friend was in this position because of Lynée's advice.

"I'll drop you off at the hotel in Cascade Creek. Keep insulting people, and see how far your investigation gets around here."

She flipped on the radio, anything to drown out the man's irritating voice.

In less than two seconds, he turned it back off. "No."

"No, what?"

"Drive me to Reed's cabin first." He held out a piece of paper with an address scribbled on it.

She chewed on the side of her cheek. This man's tone was getting worse. Hired chauffeurs were treated better than her.

"Please," he added with a sigh. "I have to secure any evidence there before I call it a night."

Lynée rolled her eyes and tried to quiet the voice in her mind that told her putting up with this guy wasn't worth it. She should just pull over and drop him off on the side of the road. Cascade Creek was only a thirty-minute-walk from this point. But it was getting darker by the minute, and the rain only increased. She didn't have the heart to leave someone outside in those conditions. Not even the insufferable Jace Ivy.

***

Jace climbed out of Lynée's car on the gravel drive, his instincts on high alert. Reed's cabin door was open, with unmistakable bullet holes in the side of the residence. The hairs on the back of his neck were screaming at him.

In a swift move, he pulled his gun from his shoulder holster inside his jacket, double-checked the bullet count in the clip, and turned to his driver.

"Stay here."

She nodded, her lips now thin and pale, much like the rest of her face. He was grateful she didn't fight him on that instruction, like she had with everything else between them.

Only a few steps toward the porch steps and Jace clearly saw an expansive dark brown stain across the rocks. Dried blood. He'd seen enough of that in his career to identify it. The gunman could still be inside, there was no way of telling how old that stain was. Then again, if someone had been shot and died there and their body already cleared away, it was unlikely the culprit had stuck around.

Jace wasn't taking any chances. Not with the cartel involved.

He slowly approached the door, standing against the side and peering in furtively. Clearing houses was something he was glad he didn't do as often anymore. But the instincts and training were still ingrained in his soul. Slowly he moved through the rooms, making sure no one was still inside. The cabin's disheveled state and upturned furniture showed some kind of altercation had happened here. The bullet holes seemed to be limited to the exterior.

Nevertheless, someone had left this place in a violent rush.

A scratching noise pulled him to a small room in the back. His heart rate escalated. With quiet steps down the hallway, the sound intensified.

Someone was back there.

He stopped at the doorframe, tightened his grip on the pistol, then peered his head inside.

A culprit skittered across the floorboards and zoomed past his feet.

He jumped out of the way and sent a curse to the ceiling. "Fucking raccoon."

Inside the laundry room, Jace spotted the trashcan the

rodent had been rummaging through, with litter scattered across the floor. He returned just in time to see the rodent scurrying down the porch steps and into the bushes.

When he was certain the cabin was empty, he returned to the front and waved Lynée inside.

She hugged herself as she walked through the front door. "No need to call the cavalry?"

"I am the cavalry." He stood in the center of the living room, making a slow circle to spot any obvious hiding places for evidence. His gaze stopped on the blonde in the open doorway.

The porchlight framed her head in a heavenly glow, making her oversized cream sweater look more like an angel's robe. Her golden-y hair might as well have been the halo; the only thing missing was fairy wings. The image made his heart swell in a strange way.

"Where do we start?" she asked.

He shook his head. "This has to be done by me. You can sit over here, away from the windows. I'll be a few minutes."

"I can't help?"

He forced himself to tear his gaze off her. "Please don't touch anything." He pulled a pair of latex gloves from his back pocket. "This place can't be compromised with your prints."

Lynée's lips pursed. "Yeah, we wouldn't want to contaminate the raccoon's paw prints."

He smirked as he searched the rest of the kitchen, looking in every drawer, under the cabinets, inside the fridge and freezer, and any other tiny spot he could think of. Thankfully, the place wasn't that big. However, by the time he was finished, he was surprised nearly an hour had passed.

"All finished." He stripped the gloves from his hands and tossed them in the trash. "Sorry, that took longer than I expected."

The woman stared out the front window from her spot on the tiny couch, while nibbling on her lower lip. Those full, pink lips that had stolen his sole attention. She had no idea how adorable she was.

"I'm all wrapped up here. Do you want to get something to eat?"

She stopped fumbling with her car keys. The way her eyes widened at his request had him looking down at his shirt. Maybe he'd dropped something on it or had left his pants' zipper down.

"Don't act all stunned," he urged again. "I'm hungry, and since you've driven me around today, I thought I'd thank you by paying for dinner. Unless...you're not hungry?"

Her expression cleared. "I'm not, actually."

His hopes dashed, and disappointment surprisingly crept in to replace them. He hid it with a lazy sigh. "Well, you're my ride to the motel, since the police lot is closed by now. The least I can do is pay for a meal. How hard is that?"

She stood, raised her chin, and looked him squarely in the eye. "I'll drive you to the motel, but I'm not interested in dinner with you."

The floorboards creaked with her every determined step on her way out.

Jace almost chuckled. *Was I just rejected?*

He followed her outside. "But I'm hungry."

"Then order takeout." She yanked on the car's door handle and climbed inside.

When he was in the passenger seat, he studied her hard expression. "Did I tick you off at some point?"

She gave him an exaggerated surprised look. "What amazing investigative skills you have. My tax dollars hard at work." Sarcasm laced every word.

"All right, enough. What did I do?"

"You're the detective." She turned the ignition, and the engine rumbled to life. "Or is that not what a Special Investigations Agent does?"

"Whatever I did," he sighed. "I apologize. You've been very helpful and accommodating. I know this has disrupted your normal routine, and that can be difficult. I assure you I will do everything I can to finish up this whole thing as quickly as possible so you can return to your regular life."

As Lynée pulled onto the main road, she licked her top lip. Her profile was even more angelic in the moonlight than earlier, and her long lashes were amplified by her glasses.

"If you hadn't started your apology with 'whatever I did,'" she began, keeping her gaze on the road, "I would've considered it as sincere, and not as just some line you memorized from sensitivity training."

He scoffed. Damn. Those *were* things he'd learned to say in his required sensitivity training. Normally they'd worked on the few other occasions he'd had to use them. This time, with her...they backfired.

"What is so offensive to you about me paying for dinner? Are you really out of practice at accepting simple thank yous?"

She chuckled, the kind that didn't sound genuine. "You're clearly out of practice at giving thank yous."

"Fine. Don't accept it then." He forced himself to look out the side window. Drumming his fingers on the dash. The sooner he got to the motel and unloaded all the evidence, the sooner he could get out of this car and do his damn job. This librarian had turned so aggravating in record time.

They rode in silence the rest of the way to the motel. Which was far too long for his liking. When she pulled into the parking lot and stopped by the lobby, he practically jumped out of the car to escape her.

The place was small, simple, and lacking the luxuries of larger hotels in major cities he was used to. An older lady with silver hair tied back with an orange scrunchie manned the check-in desk. Who was pleasant, but didn't move nearly fast enough for Jace's liking. Finally, with his room key in hand, he returned to Lynée's car. In the trunk were more bags and boxes of evidence than he could carry at once. But dammit, he'd sure try anyway.

The car switched off, and Lynée joined him at the trunk. She asked softly, "Do you really want to offer a genuine thank you?"

He stopped pulling bags from the trunk. "If it won't get my head bitten off."

"Then I'll meet you back here at eight a.m. tomorrow."

He narrowed his gaze at her, waiting for the punchline. "Why?"

"We have a case to solve."

CHAPTER 9

JACE SCRUBBED HIS teeth a little harsher than normal the next morning. That Lynée woman had driven away so fast the previous evening, he didn't have time to ask her what she meant by '*we* have a case to solve.'

Who turns down dinner so brusquely, but then wants to help investigate a case?

In his experience, it was always the other way around. From how adamant she'd been about not eating with him, it didn't make sense that she'd want to spend any additional time with him going through mountains of evidence.

Evidence that technically wasn't even his job to go through. None of this was part of his job description. He was just brought in to track and apprehend Reed Monroe. All the following hours of torture perusing this stuff was going to be self-inflicted. Without extra pay either.

Not that he was in this job for the paycheck.

He splashed cold water on his face to help wake him up. He wasn't sure how much help she'd be. She wouldn't be allowed to see most of this evidence, and the rest would be so monotonous and tedious, it would make most people's eyes cross within twenty minutes. But whatever. If she insisted on being a part of this, she could knock herself out.

He'd give her thirty minutes before she would quit and

run screaming out the front door.

He dreaded this day, further interaction with this blonde fireball. Hopefully, she didn't expect him to start walking on eggshells because she felt the need to interject herself in *his* case. Because he didn't give a damn about eggshells. This woman just seemed to have more than most people. Nothing he did was right. Fine, he was rough around the edges, but who turns down dinner?

A knock pounded his door at precisely eight o'clock.

He opened it to a bright and bubbly Lynée Clark. Wrapped in a huge gray coat with a white furry hood and matching boots. She looked more like she was ready to go skiing. A tray of steaming coffees in one hand and a bag of something that smelled like sausage biscuits in the other had him mystified.

"Mornin'. I assumed you hadn't had breakfast yet. Please tell me you're a coffee man."

"Thank you. Most law enforcement is." He pushed the door open wider for her to come through.

Three feet inside, she stopped and stared.

He followed her gaze around the room. Boxes and bags of equipment were stacked on the available desk and counter space around his tiny hotel room. He'd spread out as much as he could last night trying to find some organization, though most of what he needed was on Monroe's hard drives.

"You've been busy."

"I'm not here on vacation."

Her smile widened. "Excellent."

He cocked his head. "Why, does that impress you?"

"You're all about business here. Which means we should be able to solve it faster, and Skye and Reed can return sooner."

He scoffed. "Don't get your hopes up. I work fast and don't linger on anything, but there's *a lot* involved in this one. Won't be a quickie case by any definition."

She slipped out of her coat and draped it over his pillow.

Suddenly, this was too invasive for him. "Don't you have a day job to go to?"

"I took some time off. Wanted to put my whole effort behind this."

"Great," he muttered under his breath and shut the door.

"I brought a peace offering." Her voice was so cordial and cute. She set the food and coffees on top of a box since all the dresser space was full.

How was he going to get through this? He leaned against the door and crossed his arms. "This should be interesting." In his previous relationships, normally, he was the one expected to apologize for something.

"We got off on the wrong foot yesterday. I'm hoping this can help us start fresh. And perhaps set some ground rules."

He could feel his own eyebrows hitting his hairline. "*You* have rules?"

She moved to the other side of the room, careful where she stepped around the boxes. "I understand as a law enforcement officer, you have a certain amount of power and responsibility. You're used to doing things your way and are all about controlling the situation. I will concede to your authority in matters of this case and respect your position, as long as you remain professional and use appropriate manners."

He cocked his head the other way this time. She was so bright and optimistic, she probably had no clue she looked this damn adorable. "Have I not been professional so far?"

She paused, pursing her lips. "No."

He bit back a smile so hard, his tongue hurt. "How so?"

"You've been brash, forceful, and aggressive, with absolutely no manners. Yes, you have a job to do, but please understand I'm here to *help* you. Not be your slave."

Oh, God, help me. The image of her as his personal slave flitted through his mind, and there'd be no way for him to focus on the task at hand now.

"So, to be clear on what you're asking, you would like me to use my pleases and thank yous more often?"

Her smile never faltered, but the coldness in her eyes from last night returned for a few seconds. "And to lose the condescending tone and attitude for the foreseeable future. One catches more bees with honey than a salty demeanor."

"I'll keep that in mind if I start hunting bees. But today, I'm catching criminals and dirty agents. I'll use whatever salty vinegar I can get my hands on to finish the job."

"Fair enough. So long as you realize I'm not the criminal. I don't respond to salty vinegar. If you want the job done faster, keep the peace with the research assistant."

Now he couldn't hold back his smile. "I've never had a research assistant before."

Her bright eyes returned at that. "Well then..." She grabbed a coffee off the tray and handed it to him. "Allow me to enlighten you."

"You did say research is what you do best. Am I right?"

She winked. "You haven't seen anything yet."

***

Hours later, Lynée's back started aching. Perusing paper after paper while sitting on the double-sized bed without any back support was going to cause horrendous issues with her posture. She looked up from her stack and noticed the entire case that she and the mountainous man worked on seemed to have expanded in this tiny motel room.

He occupied the flimsy roller chair by the small desk in the corner. She doubted that thing would hold his weight for much longer.

"We need more room." She pulled her glasses off her nose.

Jace looked up from the screen on one of the laptops he'd confiscated from Reed's bags. As the hours had drawn on, his eyes had started to squint tighter and tighter. "Do what you can with what we have."

"You can't properly investigate without the appropriate space. The chat sessions from that game alone I'm reading could fill half a filing cabinet. I need to spread these out on a timeline."

Jace huffed, then rubbed his eyes. "We should stop for lunch anyway."

"I'm on a roll here, so we'll just get takeout. But first, let's move all this back to my house." She stood and rolled out the tension in her shoulders.

The federal agent froze. For some reason, that intensive stare he fixated on her seemed to elevate the temperature of the room a good ten degrees.

She swallowed, worried she may have said something off-limits. "There's so much more room. I have comfortable chairs to save our backs, and we won't be crawling all over each other just to get a file."

He tipped his head and lifted a brow.

"Do you have a better idea?" she asked.

"These aren't just library books you can check out at your convenience. This is all evidence. Which must remain in my custody until I can secure them back at the DEA. You want me to leave all of this stuff at your house, an unauthorized person to mess with as you please, which could compromise my entire investigation?"

She waved away his concern like an impatient mother to a toddler. Reminding her that he wasn't *supposed* to have outside help on his case just wasted time in her mind. In one morning alone, she'd learned just how far back Reed's investigation into the cartel had started. He and his former partner, Joe, had been viciously outnumbered, outmaneuvered, underfunded, and ultimately outgunned. Despite all their disadvantages against this cartel's digitally advanced organization, Reed and Joe were still able to cause so much havoc to their supply chain. Most of it just from behind a computer screen. And all of that just skimmed the surface. Lynée hadn't even seen any of the financials that Jace was researching. That was one area the DEA investigator was adamant she did not see.

"Think of it this way," she urged. "You won't have to keep walking to the lobby and ask the manager to borrow his printer. We can use mine."

The side of Jace's jawline twitched. Like he was chewing on the inside of his cheek. "Fine. But we're stopping for food somewhere. I'm starving."

CHAPTER 10

EMILIO SAT IN the driver's seat and lit up a cigarette. The form lying on the ground outside the Seattle motel was obscured by the drizzle on his windshield. Lovely Seattle weather.

The rain would help cover his tracks. The office manager in the lobby sported a new hole in his head as well. Both he and the housekeeping lady had seen his face. They couldn't remain alive. But he got what he came for.

At least now, he knew who he was following. With an image of both Reed Monroe's face and the blonde *gringa* he traveled with, Emilio was a step closer to fulfilling his boss's orders. Only a few hours before, he'd been at the morgue, stealing Diego's body and hiding it in a refrigerated truck bound for Mexico, driven by a trusted henchman.

A fruitless effort, in Emilio's opinion. Not that he would ever share that with Carlos Cabello. He knew better than to have an opinion when it came to the cartel boss' family. Even though Diego wasn't worth all this effort. Sure, the kid had been smart with all his fancy computers, servers, and new online game to hide their organization's supply chain. But he was cocky. Too sure of himself and greedy. Not ready to face the brutalities of the cartel's organization, despite what the man had claimed. Clearly evidenced by having his head blown off in this shoddy motel only a few days ago.

Emilio took an extra-long puff on his cigarette and let the smoke billow around his head inside the car. He wasn't here to think or have an opinion. He was here to carry out orders. Only one thing left to do before he continued on in his quest. Any second now.

He checked his watch.

A small boom burst out from the front of the motel.

Emilio glanced up.

The windows busted out of the front doors, and thick flames terrorized inside the building. Black smoke billowed into the gray skies.

The bodies would be charcoal in a few minutes. Thanks to a simple bomb using the microwave in the employee break room. The effect accelerated nicely with a few portable propane tanks from the maintenance closet.

He always loved a good bonfire.

A chime sounded on his phone. Emilio checked his text messages.

An address from his boss.

Cascade Creek, Washington.

Time for another road trip.

***

The second Lynée stepped into Rock Road Diner after loading up her car with all of Jace's evidence from his motel room, Skye's absence hit her full force. It was the first time she'd ever walked into this place without seeing her best friend behind the counter. Her brilliant smile, her infectious laughter, even the smell of her mouthwatering apple pie was missing. Lynée's heart ached from the hole inside it.

The only way to fill it was to finish this case so she and

Reed could return to Cascade Creek for good.

Jace tapped his fingers on the linoleum countertop.

No one was there to take their order. Nayanna, one of the other waitresses that Lynée had always liked, was busy talking to a group of customers at a table in the far corner, who all appeared to be complaining about the food.

Ralph yelped from behind the order window, and a large sizzle filled the air behind the wall. Followed by a bunch of curse words that hurt Lynée's ears.

She pressed her lips together. Maybe coming here was a bad idea. Without a decent cook, the diner's owner was forced to man the stoves. Ralph's food was known to drive customers away faster than a quarantine sign.

Jace chuckled. "Having a little trouble back there?"

Ralph poked his head behind the order window and scowled at the lawman. "Oh, it's you."

Jace shook his head as Ralph came around to the front counter. He grabbed a chunk of ice from the bin with his bare hand, then wrapped a rag around the fist. "I'm missing a chef, once again. Because of *you*."

Nayanna returned from the table, the caramel-colored beauty looking frazzled. She gave Lynée an apologetic smile. "Sorry about the delay. Booth or a table?"

"To go," Jace answered. "Preferably not poisoned."

Nayanna gave him a doubtful look. "No telling with this one in the kitchen." She gestured her head toward Ralph. "I know you're swamped, but Gloria and Victor said their chicken was undercooked. Can you whip up another plate?"

Ralph shot her a horrified look. "Don't say that in front of other customers! And I have half a mind to refuse service to this clown."

Jace raised an eyebrow. He glanced around the diner

with considerably fewer tables full than the first time he'd walked in. "You look like you could use the business right now."

The owner shook his head and flounced off back into the kitchen.

"What can I get for you?" Nayanna asked with a sigh and pulled out her paper pad.

"The clam chowder and a side salad please," Lynée replied.

With a discerning look, Jace crossed his arms over his muscular chest. "Gloria and Victor's chicken...was that fried or grilled?"

"Fried," Nayanna answered. She shifted in her feet.

"Is the boss better on the grill?"

The waitress shrugged. "I'm sorry to say he might burn yours on purpose."

Jace shook his head with a laugh. "Gotta love small towns. I'll take steak and eggs. Scrambled. Fries and a side salad with a tall glass of milk."

"Are you sure about that?" Nayanna paused. "A BLT and coleslaw might be safer."

"I'll take my chances. He wouldn't want to deliberately sabotage a federal agent's lunch over a grudge."

Nayanna closed her ordering pad, then glanced at Lynée. "He sure is new around here." She left to start their orders.

Lynée leaned in close to Jace so no one else would overhear. "Ralph is the kind of guy to hold a grudge a long time. If he had an ornery customer, I wouldn't put it past him to drag their hamburger buns on the floor first."

Jace took a seat on an empty stool at the counter. "I like to live on the edge."

His phone shrilled through the diner. He pulled it from

his pocket and answered gruffly. "Ivy here." As the person spoke on the other end, Jace's expression lost its playful edge. "When?" The lines across his forehead deepened. "Send me the details." He ended the call, and more dings sounded on his phone. He scrolled through notifications, his eyebrows drawing together tighter as he read.

"What's going on?" Lynée asked. "Looks like you lost your appetite."

He shoved the phone back in his pocket. "Not at all. But we need to speed this up. I have to make a trip to Seattle."

She dug around in her purse for her wallet. "Right now?"

He pulled his wallet out of his other pocket. "After we drop off all the evidence. I got this."

Nayanna returned with the check, which he paid with a credit card.

"Am I allowed to ask why?" Lynée asked quietly.

"Sure." His smile was short, clipped, and disingenuous. "You can ask."

Nayanna came back the last time with their lunches in plastic containers.

The gruff DEA agent opened his and swore a little too loudly. "Ooh, Ralph's one vindictive son of a bitch."

Lynée cringed. "What did he do?"

He turned the container around for her to see.

His beautifully cooked steak soaked in ketchup.

CHAPTER 11

LYNÉE SURVEYED HER kitchen table, covered with boxes, bags, and computer equipment. More boxes on the floor. All the evidence from Jace's motel room. He'd left only seconds after they'd unloaded everything at her house and scarfed down his ketchup-covered steak. Something pressing in Seattle, which he still refused to tell her about. Nor did he give her a timeframe when he'd return.

"You picked a fine time to leave, Agent Ivy," she said to the scattered equipment.

But something inside her glowed. She *loved* research. Even more, she loved learning new things.

This DEA case, as monotonous as the details would be, would give her a new experience outside her safe little routine. Something she would never have a chance to see otherwise if it weren't for Jace. Federal investigations and international crime syndicates. To see how these masterminds operated to hide their money and evade oversight would probably cause others to groan in agony over the tediousness. But not her. This world fascinated her.

With her sticky notes and highlighters ready, she dove into the first box. Dividing the files and papers into some sort of identifiable category was the first step. It shouldn't take her that long before she would tackle the computer files. That would probably be the most tedious work. The multiple hard drives and backups all probably held several gigabytes of data each. But at least she had the piece of paper where Reed had written down all of his passwords. Jace had left it on the table at the motel, and she grabbed it to make sure it wouldn't become lost.

She wanted to call Skye so much. The story of Ralph exacting his revenge on Jace by ruining his steak with ketchup would have her laughing for a week. Then they would've spent a decent chunk of time coming up with ways to pull a similar prank back on him. Instead of pulling off the prank, her friend would've brought something to the diner to cheer up the place, like new fresh flowers or a recipe for new pies, which would cool Ralph's jets in the process.

More importantly, if Skye could see all the evidence sitting around Lynée's house at this moment, she would smile broadly with a wink, and say "Only you would call this seventh heaven, Lynnie."

A few hours later, she finally made it to the hard drives and mentally cataloged the various files to sort through. They were even more full than she originally suspected. So many random files, not sorted as well as she'd hoped for a federal agent. A whole folder marked as Follow-Ups, another named Lexi Code, whatever that meant, and one named Christmas List.

"Wow. They either didn't sort things well, or Reed really was in a hurry to copy his stuff and run."

Three coffee pots later, her eyes started to hurt, and a slight headache threatened her temples. With a glance at the clock, she realized five hours had gone by, and daylight faded quickly outside.

Water. I need to hydrate. Maybe dinner, too. "Guess I'm eating alone tonight."

What in the world was keeping Jace stuck in Seattle for

so long?

***

Jace hunkered down in his leather jacket against the brisk wind. Seattle was somehow colder than Cascade Creek but much busier. Walking through the charred rubble of the tiny motel room, the smell of smoke still lingered heavily in the air. Jace coughed several times, his eyes filling with water. He hoped like hell to find any evidence still viable for his case.

The fire department had given him clearance to enter, even though the roof and walls were mostly missing, and only a few metal fragments remained of the supports and furniture. The police detective had given him a brief rundown of the events as they knew them, including a witness's account of seeing a dark sedan leaving the scene just after a large explosion.

Apparently, some kind of homemade bomb had gone off in the break room using the microwave and a few propane tanks as accelerants. All meant to cover up the two bodies in the lobby littered with bullet holes. Now also charred to a crisp and beyond recognition. The coroner would need dental records to identify them. But they were more than likely hotel employees.

Seeing their mutilated remains and the accompanying burnt-flesh stench didn't bother Jace anymore. Years of investigating brutal homicides and arresting the truly psychotic and evil criminals of the world as part of his job in the DEA numbed him from all that. Which was the part that bothered him. That he wasn't affected by all of that anymore.

What he was affected by was all his evidence sitting in that woman's house without him in it. Trust was not one of his fortes. And dammit, this woman had forced him into trusting people he never would've considered before. A damn suspect, among them.

He slowly turned in the small space. The mattress and furniture were all burned away, and only the metal frame remained, twisted and warped against the blackened toilet and bathtub. Large black spots marred the sheetrock. Any evidence they could've used against Monroe, or the cartel, was destroyed.

According to his DEA agent currently in hiding, this was the room in which Diego Huerta was killed. Where he'd first attacked Skye and Reed, and the cartel assassin subsequently died of a gunshot wound to the neck. Monroe also claimed this guy had been the technological genius behind Carlos Cabello's new digital era of drug distribution and human trafficking. A lofty and unlikely allegation, considering this Huerta guy wasn't on any DEA radar.

But so far, much of what Reed Monroe testified ended up true. This one was hard to ignore. He was certain this hotel's fire was related to the cartel assassin somehow. It was just too coincidental.

Twilight faded quickly with darkness filtering in through the destruction.

"Agent Ivy?" the detective called from the parking lot, his flashlight bright in the darkening skies.

He carefully stepped over scorched debris and made his way over to the younger-looking black man in plain clothes and a gray trench coat.

"I confirmed with the bank across the street, they have surveillance video of the day. They may have an image of the vehicle we can use."

"Excellent. I'd give my left nut for a decent face shot or license plate."

Minutes later in the bank, he and the detective

watched the security footage, with the bank manager standing behind them. From the camera's position, the motel's explosion was easily visible, a bright fireball blinding the shot. Shortly after, a dark sedan drove past.

The detective paused and replayed the footage over and over. No clear shot of the driver's face crossed the screen. Nor the license plate.

They viewed earlier footage to see if the car crossed the space earlier. Another dead end.

"Wait, who's that guy?" Jace pointed at the screen of a tall, dark figure walking into the motel lobby. There was no clear shot of what happened inside. A while later, a similar figure emerged from a side door and left. But in none of those shots was the person's face visible, tucked away in a gray hoodie. Any other details about him were also indiscernible because the vantage point was too far away.

"That has to be our guy. He was the last one to go inside."

"You really believe this is related to the murder in room 802 last week?" The detective pulled his phone from his pocket from an incoming notification.

"More than likely." Sadly, he couldn't share that he likely had the "murderer" in his custody. Not yet, anyway.

"You really think that Huerta guy was part of the cartel?" Everything in the man's tone conveyed doubt, as he scrolled through his phone. "Not some kind of drug bust gone bad? Most of the clientele here aren't the reputable kind."

Monroe had told him as much. Jace had yet to see definitive evidence of Huerta's connection to the cartel. But Cabello's organization was very good at covering their tracks, and much of this smelled like him.

"Well," the detective sighed at his phone. "Someone

claimed the body already."

"They released him that fast?" Jace asked. "Who?"

"The family's pastor. Father Jorge Campos."

He groaned. "Jesus, the coroner's office was duped. Son of a bitch!" He grabbed his own phone and started looking up the info.

"What? It doesn't have to be a funeral home to claim a body. It can be a pastor."

"I strongly doubt the most famous Mexican soccer player of the nineties converted to a man of the cloth and claimed Diego Huerta's body." He showed his phone screen to the detective with the goalkeeper's biography. "Carlos Cabello is an avid soccer fan. Let me guess, coroner's office didn't check I.D."

The detective swore under his breath and started making a few calls. But Jace knew all of that would be fruitless. Huerta's body was long gone by now, and they wouldn't find who really took him. Destroying this motel was sending a message.

The cartel was in Washington State and would crucify anyone to get to Monroe.

Jace needed to get back to Cascade Creek.

CHAPTER 12

DARKNESS COVERED EMILIO'S drive up the mountainside to the tiny cabin. Cascade Creek proved harder to find than he anticipated, particularly at twilight. If it hadn't been for his navigation app, he would've driven past the exit. The whole town slept quietly as he meandered his way up a back hill and turned off onto a gravel drive.

The cabin showed evidence of a firefight. The place would've been a quaint greeting-card-stereotype for a winter escape if it hadn't been for all the bullet holes across the facade.

Proof of the first two assassins' failure to capture the troublesome DEA agent.

The man had since fled—just as he'd done all the previous times he'd been found—but this cabin was the first place to capture clues as to where he'd gone. Time for old school tracking.

When he was sure no one had followed him, Emilio climbed out of the car and easily picked the lock on the front door. Inside, the compact room had been recently ransacked. Closets emptied, furniture moved around, but a fresh gallon of milk still sat in the fridge along with a few energy drinks.

The small wooden table in the kitchen sported square

dents across the top. This was where the agent had set up his computer equipment. Monroe had quite a talent for making the cartel run ragged chasing their money around the globe, all using nothing more than an internet connection. Which ultimately led to Diego Huerta's death and a huge bounty on this disgraced DEA agent's head.

Emilio continued searching the cabin, finding no clues to the man's trail. He searched through the kitchen cabinets until he came to the junk drawer.

Bingo.

A paystub. To Guy Hancock.

From Rock Road Diner.

There's my trail.

The diner was much easier to find than the cabin. The casual box-style restaurant was the newest building on the main road out of town. The front sign's lights were turned off, but still easily visible. Emilio drove past it until he found a way to the rear entrance. There didn't appear to be security cameras on the building. He smiled. Quaint towns like this were so trusting.

Picking the lock on the back door was much harder than the cabin. After a few minutes, the familiar *click* came, and the door opened.

Into a storeroom. Small, a little dusty with a strong cardboard scent. He found his way into the back kitchen and instantly crinkled his nose at the overpowering smell of cleaning solution. A large open window at the front of the kitchen revealed the eating area, all dark with a little moonlight peeking in through the blinds. To the right was the manager's office. Unlocked.

The room was so much tinier than Emilio expected. More like a bathroom stall. Barely enough room for a chair and a computer and a small safe under the counter. The papers on the desk and files in the drawers didn't give him anything to follow Monroe's trail. Just a few more paystubs and minimal info on Guy Hancock.

Emilio snarled and shoved the drawer closed.

Back in the kitchen, he stood in the doorway leading to the dining area. He scanned the area slowly, thinking...

His gaze stopped on a picture frame on the wall. Behind the front counter, was the Employee of the Month's smiling face. The same blonde woman from the Seattle motel's security footage. The one beside Reed Monroe in their escape.

The name on the picture's plaque: Skye Winters.

He smiled.

CHAPTER 13

PAPERS IN VARIOUS stacks covered Lynée's kitchen table and chairs. Multiple colors of sticky pads, highlighters, several legal pads, a half-dozen three-ring binders, and God knew what else filled the spaces in between. All this evidence probably shouldn't be at her house, but hell, Jace had already thrown protocol to the wind several times over. Lynée was good so far, and frankly, he needed the help.

She was clearly in her element, and Jace smiled at her utterly innocent and adorable nature. But damn, wasn't she thorough. And smart as a leather whip.

He set his bag with his laptop on a dining room chair. He was in such a rush yesterday to get to Seattle, he hadn't taken the time to inspect the details of her house. The walls displayed lots of picture frames and canvas paintings—handmade. Books filled the multiple shelves in almost every room. More photos, lots with her and Skye, and several with her and an elderly couple he assumed were her parents.

One frame stole his attention. Lynée in a wedding gown. A simple yet beautiful satin masterpiece, with flowers woven into her hair... Her gorgeous smile...

A bridal portrait.

But no photos of a groom anywhere.

"So, hey," she called from the kitchen, holding a

steaming mug. She once again wore an oversized sweater similar to yesterday's, this one purple. "How was Seattle?"

"Cold. You've been busy." He gestured to the table and avoided elaborating on her question on purpose. No one ever wanted to hear the gruesome details, no matter how powerful their curiosity. "Run me through what you've sorted so far."

"Care for some coffee first?"

He shrugged out of his coat, draping it over the back of a chair. "In a minute."

She cocked her head to the side, observing him with a strange look on her face. Her hair was piled into a messy bun on the top of her head, so comfortable and playful looking.

"What?" he asked.

"When on Earth do you find time to work out?"

He placed his hands on his hips and glanced down at his frame. He wore a pair of jeans and a black T-shirt, nothing fancy. Clearly, she liked his muscles. Before today, she didn't seem interested in his physique, and now she mentioned it when he's wearing casual clothes. The subtle opening intrigued him. "Most of the time early in the mornings. If I'm not...otherwise occupied."

The innuendo struck home, just as he hoped it would. She blushed.

Which had him so much more curious than ever before into what made this woman tick.

She cleared her throat and downed some coffee. Then she directed her attention to the stacks of paper. "I'm putting most of my focus on the Dark Inferno game contacts Joe and Reed followed, background checks, and putting them on my timeline." She pointed to a legal pad in front of her chair. Then she ran down the rest of the sections she'd separated out.

"Sounds good." He moved to the kitchen to make his own coffee.

"What are you going to focus on?" She followed him.

"Whatever jumps out at me." He poured a cup, ignoring the sugar and creamer. The first sip hit his system like a heating blanket on his soul.

She tapped her finger on the rim of her mug, obviously irritated by his vague answer. "I only ask, so we're not double-dipping on the same topic. It would make this whole thing take longer."

He studied the little dent on the ridge of her nose where her glasses usually sat. He'd only seen her without glasses once before, so he assumed she either only needed them for reading, or sometimes wore contacts. Did she prefer her glasses? Were contacts too much of a pain for her? Though he dared to admit he kinda liked the sexy librarian look. Which probably made him chauvinistic in some people's opinions.

"Did you hear me?" she asked again.

"Yeah." He shook the thoughts from his mind. "When you're through with the game contacts, go through the rest of the files on the other hard drives. If you come across anything financial, put it to the side. I'll need to do those."

"What will you work on?"

He grabbed his laptop bag and moved to the living room, hoping the distance would force him to focus. "Something confidential." He picked a spot at the coffee table.

Her heavy sigh caught his attention. Now she was frowning.

Great. Had what he been thinking been written all over his face?

Then he realized it. *Damn.* He'd been too dismissive with her, again.

"I'm sorry. Too direct again?"

She raised her coffee in a mock toast. "Look at that, ladies and gentlemen. He can be taught."

He smirked at her sarcasm. "I'm not used to explaining myself. I usually work alone." He set his mug on the coaster on the television stand. "I'll be looking at personnel files of fellow agents, which I can't let you see."

"Fair enough. That wasn't so difficult, was it?" She resumed her seat at the kitchen table, her hips doing a little shimmy in the chair. Like she was a kid settling down to watch her favorite movie.

He couldn't help himself, he had to smile. Which he hid behind rubbing his beard. Then dug out his laptop and set up with the screen facing away from prying eyes.

"Do you like to listen to music as you work?" she asked from across the room.

Music? Did she just ask about music? He wanted to pinch the space between his eyes, feeling the beginnings of a headache. Music was a luxury he could not afford. He was normally too damn busy on calls or following leads to turn on music. But he had to learn to play nice. "Um, sure." And frankly, if it helped her work faster, she could knock her socks off.

With a click of a remote, a few speakers around the living room softly played some pop tunes.

"Let me know if you want to hear a different station. I go through phases." With that, she tucked those black-rimmed glasses back on her nose and buried her face in her own laptop screen.

The rest of the morning passed with excruciating numbness. Jace despised investigating fellow agents. But he had to listen to his gut. With moles and missing reports, he had to go up the chain of command from both Reed Monroe and Joe Padilla. So the first person he had to investigate and comb through his employment records was their boss, John Bordowski, from the El Paso office. A Special Agent in Charge might not have the clearance to remove files in systems, but maybe he somehow found a way. More importantly, Jace needed to determine if the man had connections in the Cabello cartel somewhere down the supply chain. That meant combing through his previous cases dating back as far as his employment records went. Finding any anomalies, complaints, or transfers that appeared out of the standard operating procedures.

Because there was absolutely nothing standard about investigating superior federal agents for working for the enemy and framing subordinates for it.

From there, he'd have to dig into their personal lives, like financial records, taxes, social media accounts, and hobbies. Some things Jace just didn't want to know about his DEA brothers and sisters. One previous investigation revealed an agent he'd gone to the academy with had been cheating on his wife of twelve years while she was going through chemo for breast cancer. Jace had left that little detail out of his final report, but he could never look at the guy the same way again. A perfect example of why Jace refused to trust people.

"Hey."

He looked up from his screen. Lynée leaned against the archway between the living room and hall. The collar of her sweater dipped over a shoulder, revealing a thin strap of her undershirt. Lavender.

"You've hunkered down further in that chair over the last few hours, and your back is going to hate you. Unless you get up and move around."

As soon as she said the words, he noticed the tightness in his neck and lower back. "Crap. What time is it?" He checked his watch. Well past lunchtime.

"I could practically hear your stomach growling over the music." She smiled and moved closer, handing him a glass of water.

"No, that was my conscience."

A little V formed between her eyebrows. "Found something you didn't like?"

"Having to do this in the first place is what I don't like. Leaves a really bad aftertaste." He downed the whole glass. He wiped his mouth with the back of his hand. "Digging into people's lives makes me feel dirty. Not in a good way."

Lynée scooted some files over on the coffee table to make room to sit. "If you feel dirty, go take a shower upstairs."

Their gazes met.

"Seriously?" he asked. That was the last thing he expected this woman to offer. Well, second-to-last.

She shrugged. "There are extra towels in the closet. We'll have lunch when you're finished."

"You wouldn't mind?" Now that she mentioned it, a shower sounded great. Just to clear his head. Not as well as a ride on his bike would accomplish, but it'd do for now.

She shook her head. "I'll show you where it is." Then stood.

At the same time he rose.

Their bodies bumped into each other in the small space between the table and his chair. A strong wash of coconut scent hit his senses. His mouth watered instantly, and he realized it came from her hair. He leaned into it for a split second, just couldn't help it.

"Sorry," she muttered. She grabbed both of his arms to steady herself. Her grip on his bare skin was so soft but sure. Then she side-stepped him. A bright pink blush colored her cheeks. "Didn't realize the furniture was so close together over here." She ducked her face and started for the stairs.

He watched her move away and cursed his body's instant response to her close proximity. He set his laptop on the table where she'd just sat and tried to adjust himself so his growing hard-on would disappear. Or at least not be as visible in his jeans. Hell, had it really been that long since his last release? Barely a brush against her body, and he was like a teenager jonesing for a tussle in the sheets.

Awkwardly, he followed her upstairs and stepped inside the bathroom as quickly as he could. Just before he closed the door, he spotted her gaze darting south, and her pink cheeks shifting to a bright red.

Aw hell, might as well own up to it. "See something you like?"

She opened her mouth to say something, but nothing came out. She closed her mouth and turned on her heel to head downstairs.

Now, he had a really hard choice. Make it a cold shower or just finish on his own. Maybe that coconut soap or shampoo was in here somewhere.

CHAPTER 14

LYNÉE PRESSED A bag of frozen peas to her cheeks. And mentally chastised herself.

She'd ogled him. Outright gawked. Only to be caught and called out for it. Now she couldn't get her face to cool off.

When she'd gripped his arms to step around him so she wouldn't fall, she was amazed how each of his muscles flexed beneath her fingers. Like smooth concrete warmed from the sun after a hot summer day. For a split second, as she brushed past him in the living room, an image flashed in her mind of that strong arm wrapped around her in a heated embrace, the weight of him pushing her into a mattress, his breath hot on her neck like it was in the living room. Oh, his musky cologne had hit her in just the right way.

Now, she didn't want to return to the living room, because more than likely that scent lingered. She'd never be able to get those images out of her head.

"What is the matter with me?" It's not like she'd never seen an erection before. Her short-lived marriage with Todd had included a decent love life. She shouldn't be reacting this way. She'd been turned on before, aroused and in love with the idea of making love. But then again, with Todd, it hadn't been this...*overpowering.*

She pitched the peas back in the freezer and started making two club sandwiches. By the time Jace returned from his shower, she hoped much of the blush in her face had disappeared. His clomps down the stairs came much quicker than she expected.

Just ignore it. If she didn't bring it up, then maybe they could proceed as though it never happened. She finished their plates with a serving of baby carrots and left out a jar of pickles and other sides. His unmistakable form stepped into the archway, but she refused to look up.

"I didn't know if you preferred carrots or pickles or what. So, just pick whatever you want and dig in." She grabbed her own plate and prayed her cheeks weren't scorching red.

"Lynée," he said, his voice so soft.

The heat built in her face again. Already. She had no choice. She looked at him.

Damp hair and refreshed, with a few strands falling over his forehead, he looked like a Sports Illustrated cover for women. The rugged mountain man edition. A real-life Rhett Butler if he lived in the Pacific Northwest.

"I'm sorry if I made you uncomfortable," he announced.

She flapped her hand in the air, hoping it wasn't as shaky as her knees. "Not at all. Just biology, right?" She moved to the kitchen table and set aside a bunch of files, so they had space to eat. Certain to not glimpse at his impressive bulge. "I shouldn't have stared."

He sat across from her. "I took it as a compliment."

"I bet you did."

He lifted the bread off his sandwich and studied the inside. "Thanks for letting me use your shower. Did you come across anything with the game contacts?"

"Some." She finished chewing, thankful for the subject change. "A lot of chatter about payments and bank accounts. It would make things easier if I had visibility into some of that info to connect these individuals together."

He shook his head, putting the ingredients back together. "I can't let you see that."

"Come on. There's so much info, and you can't do it all on your own without it taking weeks and weeks. I can help wade through it to take less time. I'll sign whatever NDA you want. Place my hand on the good book and vow silence to all except you, if it helps."

He leaned his elbow on the table and stared at her. "You're willing to do all this just so Skye can return faster?"

"Of course. Wouldn't you do the same—and more—for your best friend?"

He chomped on a carrot, clearly studying her and considering the idea. Hopefully, it was enough. "All right. You must sign an NDA, and you can't print anything with bank account numbers. Not a single scrap of paper. No screenshots, and you can't save anything to a thumb drive. Got it?"

She raised her hand, a triumphant smile creeping up on her face. "On my honor."

He dug into his sandwich, resuming his usual silence.

"You have a really hard time trusting people, don't you?" she dared to ask.

He stopped chewing. "Why would you say that?"

"For starters, it took next to an act of God to get you to agree to move all this stuff to my house where we have more room. Every space you walk into, you keep your back to the walls, and you're always scanning for exits. And you sifted through your sandwich to see all the ingredients in it before you took your first bite."

He scowled. "That's just common sense. Know what's going in your body."

"What, you think I'd poison it? You did the same thing at Rock Road Diner with Reed."

"Monroe was my suspect. He had the motive to try something." He grabbed another carrot.

"And me?"

He held the carrot over his plate. It was several seconds before he answered. "No, I don't think you'd try something like that. You're too..."

She sat back in her chair, folding her hands in her lap. "Too what?"

The side of his mouth lifted like it was a joke. "Trusting."

"You say that like it's a bad thing."

"In my line of work, it kinda is." He shoved the carrot in his mouth and looked down at his plate.

"That's really sad. I believe people are mostly good."

"Unfortunately, the fact that I have my job, and that the DEA even exists are proof to the contrary."

Suddenly her food didn't taste that great anymore. How could he be so pessimistic? Being around all this negativity turned things bitter.

"So, do you like to cook?" he asked with another obvious subject change.

"Yes." She sighed. Might as well comply. She'd get nowhere with him if she kept on picking at that flaw.

"What's your favorite thing to cook?"

"I like to bake too."

"Okay, so what things do you like to bake?"

She paused a moment and stared at him, perhaps debating if she wanted to grant him the privilege of knowing these details about her.

"Because if it's chocolate chip cookies, I may move in."

She nearly cracked a smile as her jaw softened, and her eyes illuminated. "I make some of the best chocolate chip cookies in the world."

He lifted his brows. "In the world? That's a pretty grand statement, Miss Clark."

"It's simply a fact, Special Agent. Maybe if you're good, I'll make some for you."

Jace let the corners of his lips lift. "I'll bear that in mind." His plate was already empty, but damn, his mouth watered at the possibility of hot, fresh chocolate chip cookies. Or was it the continued scent of her coconut shampoo? He cleared his plate to the kitchen. He promised he'd remain professional, and he was already skirting that line if he hadn't already broken it.

They each hunkered down, him on his computer with a file to decipher, and she at the kitchen table with an even bigger stack of evidence.

His thoughts wandered back to her comment about doing anything for a best friend. And wouldn't he do the same for his. The truth was he didn't know how to answer that question. He didn't have a best friend. Hadn't had one since high school. He got pretty tight with his roommate in college, but after he'd started dating a girl seriously, they didn't connect like they once did. Since then, Jace had spent his adult life focused on his career. A career that kept him on the road the majority of his life.

He scratched the side of his jaw, working his nails through his beard to relieve the itch. Admittedly, it never much bothered him being a loner. In his line of work, it was just easier. But sitting there, staring at a bunch of crap he couldn't make sense of, he felt a small ache of wondering. What would it be like to be that close with someone, like the relationship Lynée and Skye shared? Always there for each other, even in a dark time like this.

He pounded his fingers on the keyboard a little harder. That line of thinking would only end in more disappointment. Those kinds of close relationships ended with someone leaving. Or getting hurt. And he wouldn't allow that person to be him.

Lynée's voice pulled him from his thoughts. "Hey. I can't find the financials for the cartel's first bank Reed had found . . ." She looked down at herself then back at him. "What's wrong?"

She was all bundled up like a human about to enter hibernation. With the fire going, the temperature was excellent. What's with all the extra layers? He began to sweat just looking at her. He couldn't keep quiet another minute. "Aren't you boiling?"

"I suppose. It'll cool off soon."

"Are you wearing anything under that sweatshirt?"

She nodded. "A tank top."

"Just looking at you makes me feel like I'm in a steam room." Jace set aside his laptop and made his way to her side. "Arms up."

She tossed him an annoyed look, then raised her arms.

He whipped off her sweatshirt.

Under her lavender spaghetti-strap tank top, the most incredibly rounded D-cups stared back at him. Why the fuck was she hiding something so goddamn perfect?

"Hot damn, Lynée. What are you doing hiding those gorgeous boobs under all those clothes?"

Her arms crossed over her chest and furrowed her brows. "What? My mom said 'don't advertise if you're not selling.'"

"Sure, but that doesn't mean you have to dress like an Eskimo."

"Whatever. We have work to do. Can you focus?" she asked in her precious little I'm-being-serious voice.

He leaned closer, putting one hand on the table, one hand on the back of her chair. "Lynée, when was the last time a man gave you an orgasm?"

She gasped.

Yeah, he'd absolutely shattered those professional lines he was worried about earlier. But she was just too damn ravishing to mind rules.

"Um, that's a highly personal question, not to mention highly irrelevant."

"Shit, that long." He slowly shook his head. "That's a shame. I'll tell you what..." Let's see how far she'll let me take this. He leaned closer to her ear, letting the tip of his tongue slide over its shell.

Adorable goosebumps rose on her skin, so delectable he could chase them away with his tongue. And she didn't pull away.

There was his sign. "Whenever you're ready, I offer my services. I'll stroke your pearl for you."

She's gasped. "You can't do that."

"That's what it's for. I'll give you the best damn orgasm you've had in your entire life."

Her cheeks flushed and her breath turned shallow.

"You will come so long and hard, you'll forget what day it is. And your body will beg for me to do it again the next day."

Her hand clutched her tank top at the neckline. She cleared her throat. "I certainly appreciate the offer, but really that isn't necessary." She sounded just like his sixth-grade teacher —always too polite, in control, and one step away from talking down to a student.

Jace inhaled her sweet scent one last time and rose, his smile quickly turning into a chuckle. "Okay, Bell, I'm all ears. Something about a bank. Whaddya need?"

CHAPTER 15

WORKING THIS CLOSE to Jace was beyond distracting. When he was around, her thoughts were discombobulated. This guy was one-hundred percent bad boy, and Lynée was only working with him to help her best friend.

Jace had no right to smile at her like that. And those muscles. He could probably lift her up with one hand and throw her into the neighbor's yard.

Did he lick me? Yes, yes, he did. The warmth of his tongue on her ear felt too good to pull away like she should've. Unabashedly broke the rules of professionalism and decorum between them. Then his words...the promise of making her climax whenever she was ready. *Stroking my pearl.* God in heaven! There wasn't enough chocolate in the world to satisfy the craving he'd just kindled in her. A craving she had no idea was even there anymore.

But they were here to work. Not throw themselves at each other.

Besides, he was not her type, not by a long-shot.

So why did her body somehow think he was?

"This first bank is wonky. Payments to an off-shore account every quarter that seemed to have stopped three years ago. A year later, a different bank had these same payments going to a separate off-shore account, but stopped six months ago." She pointed to a spot on the computer screen.

"I bet Cabello has dozens of off-shore accounts to help run his business and stay off our radar."

"Probably, but this second bank account is also the same one where all the money from that online gaming app was deposited."

"Wait, what?" Jace leaned closer to the screen.

"The Dark Inferno game. People pay for upgrades and advanced features in the program. All that money goes into this same off-shore account."

"Why would he use the same account?"

Lynée shrugged. "Beats me. I'm more curious about these payments. The nature of it. The same amount like clockwork." She bit her lip and glanced at the timeline in her notebook. "I should probably start a new thread. See what happened on those dates."

"Sounds like a plan. Before you start that, though, how about we break for dinner? Want me to go out and grab something?"

She pushed her glasses back in place and looked up at him, towering over her at the computer. "Um, I have food here."

"Yeah? Whaddya have? I can eat a lot." He flashed that smile again.

"Well, I made a roast that we just need to heat up." She pushed back on the chair, and he stepped to the side.

He followed her into the galley kitchen. There might barely be enough room for them.

She pulled her roaster from the fridge and set it on the counter. She retrieved two plates, a knife, and a cutting board.

She lifted the lid, and the incredible smell of the beef flooded his nostrils and made his mouth water. Just like when his mom cooked pot roast. The way Dad gushed made his mother feel so proud.

"What can I do?"

She gazed at him. "Do you like wine? There's a bottle of red over there." She pointed with her chin. "And glasses are in that cabinet."

He sidled past her, but she remained focused on cutting the beef.

He returned and leaned over her shoulder, glancing into her pot. "Hot damn, woman. That's a lot of food. You expecting company?"

"Um, yeah, you."

"I mean somebody else. You feeding a husband somewhere?"

The utensils paused over the food. She looked up at him.

"I noticed your bridal portrait in the living room, but no groom."

She frowned and continued spooning gravy over his plate. "This enough?"

"That's good for starters."

She turned, placed the food in the microwave, and started on her plate. Not nearly the amount she gave him.

He handed her a glass of red wine and took a sip from his glass. "There's a story there."

"A long and...boring one." She stood by the microwave, waiting for it to finish heating up the first plate.

"That's a shame. Marriage should be anything but boring."

The slightest tilt of her eyebrow proved she agreed. "I assume you've never been married."

"No wife would ever put up with my work schedule."

"Marriage too boring for you?"

He smirked through another sip of wine. "We were talking about you. Any boyfriends? Someone special to help you consume all this food?"

The microwave finally dinged, and she switched out the plates. "Nope. Just you. So eat up."

"Why no boyfriend?"

Her dainty fingers held the glass at its stem as she sipped. "Just haven't found one. Too busy with work. Like you."

He chuckled out loud. "Bell, you are too cute for your own good. I bet you have a bunch of little boyfriends all over this town, following you around like lovesick puppies. 'Lynée, can I carry your books? Lynée, what self-help manual would you recommend for getting a woman's attention? Will you help me start a book club?' Any excuse they can come up with to be near you."

She bit her lips between her teeth, failing to hide her smile. "Don't forget 'Lynée, do you want to come to church with me on Sunday?'"

He cackled. "That's a good one. I mean, who the hell can turn down the church?"

Her eyebrows pulled together. "Holy moly." Then she spun around when the microwave went off.

"What's the 'holy moly' about?"

She carried their plates to her round wooden kitchen table. "You swear a lot."

"What the hell do you mean?"

She winced. "*That's* what I mean. Why do you have to cuss so much?"

"You probably think people who curse a lot are savages or uneducated. I'll have you know I graduated from The

Citadel with honors."

She pointed up with her index finger. "Ah, military boys are known for swearing."

He stepped closer, intentionally crowding her with the heat emanating from his body. "So are alpha males."

Her throat worked to swallow. She snuck out of his shadow to take her seat. "Let's eat."

"Bell, look at it this way. Cursing is primal."

She lifted her brows at him over her eyeglasses, watching his every move as he took the spot next to her.

He shoveled in a bite of beef and potato, not bothering with his cloth napkin. "When an animal is in pain, it howls. When a child is in pain, it cries. When an adult is in pain, he or she swears. It's a primal reflex. Shouting out 'fuck' helps to dissipate the pain."

"Goodness, Jace." She shook her head.

His grin went from ear to ear.

"What?" She paused mid-bite.

"That's the first time you called me Jace, and hot damn, baby, I love it."

She pointed at him. "Uh-uh. You don't get to call me baby. It's derogatory."

"Sorry. Hot damn, Bell."

She lowered her head back to her dinner. "Well, your theory may be correct, but here, in this house, you can't tell me you were in pain. So is it really necessary to curse so much?"

"All right. Think of it this way. Cursing can also be persuasive. It can show passion. And passion's a good thing, right?"

The corner of his lip pulled up. Like he tried to use any topic to make fun of her. How did this conversation take such a turn? Lynée simply nodded and focused on the roast.

"It can also show power," he continued. "Even for a woman, Bell. In other words, if a woman has power, she doesn't need to trade it for sympathy, nor should she."

"Why would I need sympathy? Just because I'm a woman?"

"Of course not."

"And according to your rationale, swearing is the primary way to show power? What about mercy? Like in Count of Monte Cristo. He plotted and fought for years for power over those who wronged him, only to show mercy in the end upon the realization he didn't need vengeance. Isn't that real power?"

"I never said it was the only way to show power. But it is *one* way. My point is you don't have to yield to the stereotypes of the 'fairer sex' or being 'ladylike.' Take ownership of your passion."

She openly stared at him as he took another sip of wine. That might be the most insightful thing she'd heard all year.

"In fact, at some point, my green-eyed Bell, you will swear for me." He scooped another bite into his mouth.

She shook her head, secretly liking the nickname he gave her. "Oh, no. No, I won't."

"You don't have to use the F-word, but maybe 'damn' or 'hell.' You'll see."

The warmth in her cheeks crept to her neck and across her chest.

"But, you're changing the subject." He got up to help himself to another plate of food.

"I did?"

"Sure did. I was asking about your boyfriends. Spill the beans."

Oh geez. Did she have to? She inhaled deeply. "The groom missing from those pictures is Todd. I was twenty-four, he was twenty-five. Love at first sight, cliché as it is." She took a bite, and he waited patiently.

"Not all-consuming kind of lustful passion displayed in most movies, but the comfortable love. Safe. Felt like coming home. We had so much in common: books, church, common upbringings, love of crossword puzzles. Anyway, after dating ten months, he proposed. Our families were thrilled. We got married at Saint Mary's and moved in here."

She sipped her wine. Retelling the story wasn't the hard part. It was the humiliation at the end that killed her. Reliving the embarrassment. "I was so happy. I had everything I wanted. Ready to start a family, the whole Hallmark card come to life. I thought Todd was happy too."

"Oh shit."

"It's not what you think." She picked at a dent in her table. "We were married about two years. Todd came home one day and threw me a curveball. He said he wanted to do mission work. In Kenya."

Jace's eyebrow rose. "Africa?"

She nodded. "He said he had a calling. God had spoken to him and told him to help the poverty-stricken in Kenya. As his wife, he assumed I would go with him. He never bothered mentioning this to me while we were dating. Maybe we should have waited longer before tying the knot," she mumbled. The regret over her foolishness was still raw.

"Anyway, I told him I couldn't go. I didn't have the same calling. My life is here. I love this town, the mountains, the people. The thought of sharing a life here, raising our kids here, brought joy to my heart. It was all I ever wanted."

"Did Todd know that?"

She nodded again. "I guess he just assumed that dream

could come true anywhere. Maybe it could've. I prayed over it for a long time, and in the end, I couldn't do it. But I also didn't have the heart to force him to stay."

She fought the foolish tears that threatened to shed. She was done crying over the man. He was long gone and not coming back, and she'd made peace with it.

"How long ago did he leave?"

"Two years ago."

"What about the boyfriends since then?" He swallowed the last of his meal and sat back, spinning the stem of his wine glass in his long fingers.

"Boyfriends? Nope, none of those."

His eyes narrowed to slits. "No one? C'mon, Bell. Surely, there was a man, at least one that wined and dined you, perhaps a little dessert afterward?" He wiggled his eyebrows.

She leaned over and smacked his bicep, surprised she didn't hurt her hand. "That is not my style."

"Wait." He sat forward. His face a mere twelve inches from hers, his espresso-colored eyes so deep, like he could see straight through her soul. "You were with one man? Only one? No one before, and no one after?"

Her cheeks warmed, she was sure they were beet-red.

Jace got down on a knee, swiveled her chair, and pulled her square in the front of him.

Her breath hitched. She should be scared half to death, but instead, she only felt intrigued.

"Bell." His hands gripped the wooden chair, the heat radiating to her thighs. His eyes so intense. "I'm sorry this happened to you." He shook his head. "You are a woman any man would give his left nut to be with." He pitched forward to whisper in her ear. "I would spend any possible free second making you feel like the queen you are."

Her breath stalled. His hot breath on her skin did crazy things to her, sending tingles through her whole body.

"Making you feel every inch the woman you are. A man should crave a woman like you. Want to give her everything he had. Want to give her unending pleasure and passion just because she agreed to grace him with her presence."

She exhaled a shaky breath like it was her last. Dear God. How could this man do this to her? This rough, foul-mouthed pile of tattooed muscle made her feel like her lady-parts were about to combust?

Intensity radiated off him like a pulsing sun. She expected him to lean in and kiss her any second. But he didn't. Instead, he rose.

"Enough for tonight. I'm gonna head out. I'll be back at nine in the morning. I'm gonna try to log in and see if I can't pull any old reports Joe may have filed that are still in the system." He set his plate in the sink, pecked the top of her head like he would to his sister or mother, and grabbed his leather jacket and helmet.

"I know you rarely lock your door, but you need to start now." He sent her a wink as he closed the door behind him.

She stared at the empty entryway, breathless, her plate nearly untouched.

What was that?

CHAPTER 16

WHAT THE HELL was he thinking?

Jace slipped on his leather jacket, his mind on a runaway train of thoughts. Lynée's ex should've been honest with her when they were dating that he'd had dreams that didn't involve this tiny town. For her, it was home. He couldn't just come in and expect her to drop her life here, her dreams, for such a major move.

No doubt, she was better off without the bastard, but the story pulled on Jace's insides and twisted them like a knotted rope.

He swallowed hard. *What is this woman doing to me?*

This whole tangent was not essential to completing his task at hand.

Fuck! He should've just told her *no* when she "offered" to help. He'd always worked alone and for good fucking reason.

Sure, if he was honest with himself, every word he'd said to her was true. He would frickin' worship her body. A body like hers, hiding under mounds of clothing, needed to be pleasured. But shit, did he need to say it out loud?

He may have had a fantasy or two about Lynée, but seriously, telling her any of this shit was problematic.

Ivy, you need to keep your head in the game. Quit

staring at the blonde librarian.

Did this back-woods town have a gym? Jace needed to work off this excess energy. *Then,* maybe he could focus.

He drove to his motel, Cascade Creek Suites. He wouldn't call them suites, but the bed was comfortable—big and plush.

No, he yelled at himself. *No thinking about beds.*

He changed his clothes and pulled up directions to the local YMCA. Perfect.

He scanned the parking lot before strapping on his helmet. In about two hours, he'd be covered in sweat without a thought in his head except the burn of his muscles stretching their limits.

***

Morning came too soon. He tossed and turned all night, probably jacked up on testosterone from his workout. At least he hoped that was the cause. He didn't dare admit it could be from anything else, like a woman. One in particular.

Find the mole, nail the cartel, and get your ass back to Detroit, Ivy. That's all you need to focus on.

He studied Monroe's files on the cartel's finances, one line item blending into another between all the dummy corporations and off-shore accounts. The man had apparently moved Cabello's money around the world so many times, having them chase their cash for months. Impressive for a guy as young as he was. But this Huerta character was always on the DEA's tail and wreaked plenty of his own havoc.

Jace didn't mind research, and the real smoking gun was always in the details. But this level of minutiae was daunting. Would've driven him crazy in just a few hours.

This guy had managed it for years.

When Jace arrived at Lynée's doorstep, he could smell the cinnamon from outside.

She opened the door, her hair down and curly. Like a Blake Lively look-alike. Dressed in jeans and an oversized sweatshirt, again, that covered most of her body. Nothing for him to look at, nothing for him to think about.

Good move.

"Come in," she spun toward the kitchen, leaving the door open. "I'm making French toast."

"You're making breakfast?" He closed the door behind him and followed her.

She grinned. "Every day. Don't you?"

He gave her a don't-sass-me look. "What's that?" He leaned over her stove to some thick liquid in a pot.

"Maple syrup."

"You make your own maple syrup too?" Dang!

"You sound surprised. It's not that hard. Are you hungry?" She scooped up several slices, handing him the plate and a ladle for the syrup.

"I wasn't, but this smells too good to pass up." He helped himself, ladling on the hot maple syrup like it was ambrosia.

"Just push some of those papers aside. I'm going to borrow a six-foot folding table from the library so we can spread out all our files."

He moved some stacks to the floor and glanced around her space.

She'd rearranged some things in her living room and taped a bunch of papers to the windows, like trying to use the glass as a makeshift timeline. The way she'd organized the room, she meant business. Like a new obsession.

He felt a pang of regret at how this case was affecting

her life. It wasn't her job; it was his. "Look, you don't have to do all this." He motioned with a flick of his thumb.

She took a seat at the table. "Whaddya mean? Of course I do. I told you. Skye and I are like sisters. She needs help, so I help." She poured orange juice in two glasses. "Speaking of which, I'd like to borrow the phone, so I can call her today?"

He dropped his fork. "What?"

Lynée's shoulders slumped. "I need to talk to her."

"About what?"

"About anything. Everything. Does it matter?"

"Yeah," he said, perhaps firmer than he'd intended. But Lynée was one card shy of a full deck if she thought he was just going to let her have a little girl-chat when they were supposed to be in hiding.

"We talk every day."

"It's only been two days," he retorted.

Her little Tinkerbell lips pursed together, and her eyes widened like she was about to blow. "Look, if not today, then when? What if we have questions about the case? What if we need to bring them food? I need to talk to my friend, dammit. "

His eyes widened.

Her hand flew over her mouth. "Oh no," she mumbled behind her palm.

"Lynée Clark, did you just cuss?"

Her face was the color of rhubarb when his mom would make a fresh pie every spring. She didn't say a word.

"I told you," he strung out the words. "You would cuss for me one day. Didn't have to wait long for you, did I?"

She lowered her hand. "Oh, my goodness. I need to go to church."

He busted out laughing. This adorable little librarian

had never sworn a day in her life, he'd bet. Two days with him had the swear words flyin'. "I'm so proud of you," he said between his belly laughs.

"No. No, don't be proud of me." Her head shook vigorously, her lovely locks itching for him to rein them in a wrap of his fingers.

With an elbow on the table, he leaned in closer. "I'll tell you what. You've been very convincing. I'll grant you a five-minute phone call, but *after* we get some work done."

Her eyes lit up at his words. Why that made him so fucking happy, he couldn't say. He shoveled in a bite so he could focus on something else besides those perfect pink lips.

Lynée swished the warm, sudsy water around the pot in the sink, and let their plates dry on the rack on the counter. Jace read several reports she stumbled onto in Reed's hard drives listing addresses of drop points and cartel safe houses Joe had identified last year on the border of Mexico and El Paso. One of which coincided with a human trafficking raid conducted by ICE, according to a news article she'd come across. In and of itself, that was nothing earth-shaking. But something about this article— the timing of the raids— and how it coincided with increased payments into the online gaming app's shell companies had Lynée wondering. So she kept it open on her laptop as she stayed in the kitchen.

Creating distance between her and Jace was a good thing. After his little disclosure the day before and the promise he made if she only gave him the go-ahead, she knew she couldn't be too close to him. He was scary. There, she'd said it. Not in a way where she feared for her life, but she feared for her body.

Criminy! His words, his mere presence sent a current of electricity through her body that should not be. Simply should not be.

Sure, he was a man, and she was a woman, so perhaps on some base level, there could be an attraction. But that was it—Lynée did not find him attractive. Beyond his insane muscles and confident smile, she couldn't find anything attractive about the man. He could be rude and demanding and bossy. Not to mention his lack of tidiness and his potty-mouth.

She just wished he hadn't whispered those things in her ear. A chill raced up her spine.

"This could be something," Jace called from the living room.

She looked up from her diligent scrubbing of the countertop. "You think so?"

"Yeah. It definitely sounds like a connection. More proof that Cabello has his hands in many more pockets than I expected. I'm gonna mark this page. Good work." He didn't look up at her, but that was probably a good thing.

They worked through the morning, trying to piece together the sequence of events as best they could. Lynée cut up yellow index cards for each significant event with the cartel, white cards for Joe's activities, blue for Reed, and green for DEA stuff in general. She labeled them and pinned them in chronological order to the corkboard.

Around one o'clock, he stepped back and looked at their progress. With his hands on his hips, his stare scanned from one side of the wall to the other, and his brow furrowed. Like he'd just discovered a darker secret.

What's that look about?

"What's wrong?" she asked. She moved closer, trying to see whatever the secret was from his angle. He was a good foot taller than her, and once again, his husky cologne hinted her way. If he kept his gaze on the window, maybe he wouldn't see her leaning in to smell more of it.

He looked down at her. "Nothing. Absolutely nothing. This is amazing. You could work for the government, Bell."

Why does he keep calling me that? She secretly loved it. "Oh, I don't think so. I'm quite happy where I am. Remember," she glanced from the board to him, "research is what I do."

His eyes twinkled at her like they were smiling.

It was seriously unnerving.

"Well, it's after one." She forced herself to step away. "We should eat, then we can swing by the library for that table."

"Yeah." He cleared his throat. "Do you happen to have another one of these cork boards?"

"Well, I don't, but I know where we can borrow one."

He grinned at her. "That'll work. Let's go. I'll buy us lunch. You know a good place we can go? And, uh...not Rock Road Diner."

She smirked. Yeah, Ralph wouldn't probably poison their food this time, for sure. For every day that passed without his chef and head waitress, their boss would likely up the ante on his pranks. "Let me get my purse."

CHAPTER 17

AFTER SOME "HOME cooking," as Lynée described it, at Margie's Buffet Restaurant, they headed to the library to pick up a plastic folding table. Jace rubbed his stuffed belly. Roast beef, baked chicken, mashed potatoes, and two different fruit pies. The food was so stinkin' good, he would certainly be going back there.

Lynée led the way past several rows of bookshelves. A strong scent of old books filled the air, reminding him of high school, only this library was more brightly lit. Arriving at the large, circular check-out desk, they were greeted instantly by a tall, gangly kid. Really, that's the first word that came to Jace's mind. The boy was likely in his twenties, but he had the face of a teenager. His eyes sparkled when Lynée approached.

"Hi, Lynée." He was practically bouncing on his toes by this point.

"Hi, William. I'm gonna pick up the six-foot table from the storage closet."

"Oh, right. Bernice told me you'd be coming by. How's it going? Will you be returning to work soon?" William only glanced Jace's way as he leaned closer into Lynée, his eyes dilated and his cheeks turning a little pink.

"I'm not sure." She shrugged nonchalantly. "I've got a

big project to finish first."

She had turned to walk away when William spoke. "I hope it isn't too much longer. We've missed you around here."

Jace wanted to laugh. He could see who missed Lynée the most. His earlier prediction was right on target.

As the librarian walked away, William's gaze switched over to Jace, where all his goo-goo vibes vanished. His lips thinned like he tasted rancid coffee.

Jace followed her to the dark closet. She flipped on the light switch and pointed to the white table leaning against the wall.

"Looks like Lynée has an admirer." He leaned in close as he grabbed the handle of the folding table.

She raised her gaze to him. "What are you talking about?"

He motioned with his head. "That kid out there, William. He's got a crush on you the size of Mount Rainier."

She wrinkled up her precious little nose. "No, he doesn't. We just work together."

"Bell, I'm telling you. He's crushing on you. Hard." With that, Jace hefted the table and walked out toward the front of the library. "Thanks, William," he called. "I'll try and have Lynée back to you as soon as I can."

The boy sat taller and smiled from scrawny ear to ear. "Do you need any help?"

"I got her, buddy." Jace winked at him. He let the implied meaning sink into the kid's head while they finished carrying the table outside. He couldn't help teasing just a bit.

At the car, Lynée stomped her little feet as she clicked open the trunk lid, then smacked his upper arm.

He hid the laughter bubbling up. God, she was so

fucking adorable. "Ow. What was that for?"

"You can't lead on poor William like that. I have no interest in him. That is so unprofessional."

He slammed the trunk lid and slid into the passenger's seat. "Well, maybe you should. It's been a while, Bell. I mean, the boy is sitting in there right now with a woody, dying to see you again. I bet he's never made a girl come, but you could teach him, right?"

She smacked him again. "Ah! Shut your pie hole."

He laughed. His belly quivered, and it felt good to play with her.

She started the car. "Can we just focus on our task here and getting my friend out of hiding?"

"Yes, ma'am." He turned to the window to hide his chuckling. She was cuter when she blushed. Getting her all riled up like this was almost as fun as...

Easy, Ivy. He couldn't go down that road. But damn, stashed under all that clothing, she hid some sexy assets. Poor little William wouldn't have a clue how to please her. What buttons to push, and how to edge her to that moment just before release. Hell, he'd likely blow his load the second she stood completely naked before him.

Lynée lowered her window a crack, despite the chilly air. Obviously, she was feeling the heat from their conversation just as much as he was. What was that woman thinking right now? Was she looking down the same road he was? Flirting with the idea of taking him up on his offer?

Or considering the idea of helpless William?

God, he hoped not.

No, she needed to find a man who knew how to please a woman. A man who knew what she wanted even when she didn't know herself. Most importantly, she needed a man who could commit. One who could give her the world she craved, give her babies, and devote his undivided attention to her.

He knew he fit that description. Well, most of it. The commitment part would be the dealbreaker for him. But it was still entertaining to think about.

Lynée had called Wanda at Saint Mary's earlier, asking to borrow the corkboard she knew they had sitting in the office. Unfortunately, the call had rolled to voicemail, so she had no idea if it was even okay to borrow it.

As they walked past reception, toward the main office, she heard voices. Distressed ones. She glanced up at Jace, and the look on his face told her he heard it too.

They turned the corner, and several people stood in the church's small library. More like a converted closet with the door removed and books lining all the shelving units.

"Hey, guys. What's going on?"

Wanda, Father Richard, and everyone else looked her way, stares darting to Jace. She stepped into the room and scattered there on the floor in a tumbling pile laid books. Hundreds of books.

She gasped. "What happened?"

Fr. Richard stooped down to pick up a few of the hardbacks.

"The bookcase collapsed," Wandra replied. "I think a shelf broke, and that caused a domino effect. The rest tumbled." She picked up a copy of *The Velveteen Rabbit*, the front cover broken, and the back half crushed.

Lynée's heart crumpled in on itself. She'd loved that book as a child. The library's copy looked older than hers. Her mind instantly went through her own inventory, trying to figure out which ones she could donate to replace anything unusable.

"I simply don't know what we're going to do," Wanda continued. "We just used up the available funding to replace the fencing around the church, and the rest went toward the children's Christmas play."

Jace and Lynée leaned down to stack books and assess the damage.

He grabbed a few of the broken shelves that had actually splintered in several places. "It doesn't look like this old bookshelf can be repaired."

Fr. Richard shook his head. "I'm just grateful no one was in here when it happened. They could've been hurt."

"What's the plan with the old fence panels outside?" Jace spoke.

Lynée furrowed her brows. "What?"

Fr. Richard straightened, pushing his rimless glasses back on his nose. "We're waiting for the city to come and collect bulk trash. They said it would be next week.'

Of course Jace would notice stuff like that. She had no idea what he was talking about, but clearly, with his job, he was trained to notice random details.

"I can build a bookshelf out of the old lumber. Do you have an electric saw and some tools?"

She blinked several times. Did she hear that right?

"You're a carpenter?" Wanda and Fr. Richard asked in unison.

He shrugged a shoulder. "Not officially. But bookshelves are easy."

Lynée remembered her manners. "Oh, sorry. This is Jace Ivy."

"That's awfully kind of you, Jace." Fr. Richard beamed. "That doesn't impose on you too much? There are a lot of books."

"Not at all. It won't be fancy, but from the looks of the

panels, it'll be plenty sturdy. Where are your tools?" he asked.

"Follow me."

Fr. Richard led the way out of the room.

Lynée was silenced. Jace just didn't seem the volunteer-type. That was such a kind offer, and it seemed so unlike him. Most of their time had been spent bickering, and him being so crotchety, demanding, and Scrooge-like. Except for a few moments of what she could only deduce was cabin fever getting the better of them.

"Your friend is very kind." Wanda broke her train of thought.

"It seems so," she replied with a smile. *Surprisingly kind.*

Wanda and Lynée stayed on their knees for almost an hour, cleaning up and organizing the mess on the ground as best they could. Jace had returned once to get the tall side pieces which sustained no major damage.

"Why don't you take some water out back to the shed in case the boys are thirsty." Wanda smiled at her, straightening the pile of children's books that threatened to topple over again.

Lynée held back a chuckle. Fr. Richard was probably seventy, and although he was in good shape, she would hardly call him a boy. But Wanda was even older, so everyone was probably "boy" or "girl" to her.

She followed Wanda to the breakroom and pulled out a few bottles of water.

Lynée walked out of the church's back door and across the yard to the shed. The power saw whirred from inside. She could imagine the entire place covered in sawdust. She stepped through the door, ready to cover her mouth and nose from all the debris in the air. Her shoes crunched over the wood shavings on the floor.

Nothing prepared her for what she witnessed.

Jace...shirtless.

Her mouth went dry.

Sweat covered his arms and back. Under a few pieces of sawdust on his skin, his muscles flexed as he pushed the power saw through the board.

They didn't seem to notice her, and she couldn't make her legs move. The extent of his tattoos stunned her twice-over. An intricate masterpiece of a metal shield encompassed between two giant axes, all encircled with dark ivy in curly designs countering the appearance of strong steel.

When the saw stopped, she inhaled and pasted on a smile. "How's it going?"

Fr. Richard set a newly cut piece of lumber on a stack with some others. "Hi, Lynée. Jace is powering through this project like it's nothing more than cardboard."

She nodded. Still glued to the spot.

Jace turned. He gave her a look that could only be described as a smolder. Or maybe he was just thirsty.

"Is that for me?" he asked.

"Huh?" She glanced down at the bottled waters in her hands. "Oh, yeah." She moved closer, handing one to each of them. It was then that the necklace around Jace's neck caught her eye. A thick stainless steel chain with a silver cross.

He's religious? Can't be. Not with the way he spoke and the feelings he invoked in her. The proposition he made...

He chugged most of the water and retrieved another board to set on the sawhorses for cutting.

"So, okay. You guys need anything else?"

From his position over the slab of wood, Jace turned his head. "I'll need to go to the hardware store for supplies," he announced.

"Okay, I'll be ready when you are."

He nodded, and the saw came to life.

She pivoted to leave. There were a handful of times in Lynée's life when she was truly shocked. When Todd wanted her to move to Africa, when Mrs. Latham, who opened the library, announced her retirement, and now, seeing Jace bareback. The sheer size of him would intimidate anybody. His muscles were impressive. She had no idea the male form could look so incredibly powerful. Well, of course, she did from movies and all the magazines in the library. But she'd never seen it in person.

She licked her lips as she walked back to the library. Grateful for the chillier air on her cheeks. She grabbed two more bottled waters, one for Wanda and the other for herself. Hydration could help cool these jets.

"How're they doing back there?" Wanda tilted her head when Lynée walked in.

"Um, good." She spared Wanda all the interesting details, handing her a bottle of water. "Jace wants to go to the hardware store soon."

"Thank you. I've sorted the books into piles by subject. I was going to sort each stack by author alphabetically, but my knees can't be on the floor much longer. I'm sure as a librarian, a non-alphabetical sort makes you cringe."

"Very funny."

The broken wood had been removed. All they had to do was wait for the new bookshelf, and they could reassemble the room.

"So tell me," Wanda lowered her voice and leaned in closer. "What's with the tall drink of wake-me-up out there?

Why is he here? With you?"

So many questions overloaded Lynée's brain. Mainly because she didn't know how to answer them. Wanda wasn't exactly a gossiper, and she liked her a lot for that. But something as unusual as a DEA agent in their tiny town searching for a suspect was certainly going to be too irresistible for Wanda to keep to herself. Besides, Lynée wasn't sure how much of Jace's presence and intentions were available to share with everyone else. Then again, he wasn't necessarily discreet at the Rock Road Diner the first day he was here. But with Skye and Reed in hiding, it was probably best for her to be a little more discreet.

"He's an investigator. Helping the Sheriff's office on a case."

Wanda's eyes nearly popped out of their sockets. "Really? Are you escorting him around town or something?"

Lynée tried to think of something. "Not exactly. Just one of those right-place-right-time situations."

Wanda grinned. "Oh, honey...you're telling me." She fanned herself.

She has no idea.

CHAPTER 18

LYNÉE CARRIED THE church's cork board to the side door, staring at the brown cork, worn with plenty of holes. Her mind wandered to the image of Jace's naked back and chest. No matter how badly she wanted to keep her thoughts on the case and which files she would dig into next, the man's demi-god like muscles and tattoos had hijacked her mental functioning. She'd never been that into a guy's physical appearance as much as their humor, kindness, and intelligence. That was her trifecta. But he certainly got her attention this time and rendered her speechless in that shed. Something she'd rarely encountered in her life. Practically aphasia.

Masculine voices carried on the air from the back. Jace and Fr. Richard walked toward the parking lot.

Jace had donned his shirt, pendant beneath the neckline, with his jacket in his hand. With only a cursory glance at Lynée, he addressed Fr. Richard again. "We'll run to the store and be back shortly."

"I can't tell you how much I appreciate all this." They shook hands.

He lifted the board and made his way to her car.

She followed him. "We can go to Elliott's. They have just about everything. It's only a few miles away."

"Okay," he replied as he slipped the corkboard in the back seat, then folded himself into her little car.

"Thanks for helping with this project."

"No problem." He kept his gaze out his side window.

Man of few words and she had a *million* questions.

Why won't he look at me?

She licked her lips yet again. "So, I noticed your necklace. A cross."

"Uh-huh."

"I didn't know you were religious."

"I'm not."

Gees. Like getting blood from a turnip.

"Must mean something to you then."

He exhaled. "My mom gave it to me. It used to be my dad's."

"Used to be?"

He rubbed the back of his neck. "My dad was an agent. Killed in the line of duty when I was fourteen. A drug-bust gone bad."

Her heart dropped a little. "Oh, I'm so sorry."

He adjusted the vents in front of him for more air. "This line of work ain't for the faint of heart."

She stopped at a red light, and the silence between them carried. She couldn't imagine not having her parents growing up. True, they now lived in Florida for health reasons, but she still talked to them a lot.

"It's nice you have a memento of him like that. One you can carry with you wherever you go."

The light remained red for a long time, during the continued awkward silence. He finally answered, just as the light turned green. "I didn't actually wear this for a long time after. Mom gave it to me at his funeral, but I was angry. Chucked it and blamed him for putting himself in that position. She stashed the cross away and gave it to me again before my first DEA interview. I landed the job and never took it off."

Lynée glanced his way. "It must have been hard growing up without your father."

He cleared his throat. "Why do you want to talk about this?"

"I thought nothing scared you."

"I'm not scared." He rolled his eyes. "It's just pointless."

"Why is it pointless?"

"Cuz we can't go back and change anything. I became a troubled teen. Made some bad decisions—hanging out with the wrong crowd, venting my anger in stupid ways. Nearly ended up in juvie a few times."

She had to stop again for a crossing guard leading elementary students through the crosswalk. "What set you straight?"

"My dad's partner. Phil. Told me my father would be rolling over in his grave with the shit I was pulling. If I didn't start putting my energy toward good, he'd personally see me shipped off to military school. The kind in the woods with no modern plumbing." He chuckled as if reminiscing some absurd conversation. "Anyway, I listened. And here I am."

"Here you are," she echoed. "Dedicating your life to the same public service as your father."

He nodded.

The school zone finally ended, and she pulled onto the main road with all the big box retailers. "Between all your hoodlum and troubled adolescence, where did you learn carpentry?"

"Phil. He was a big fan of working with your hands."

"Is he still with the DEA, too?"

"Yeah, but stuck behind a desk. I still talk to him regularly. He taught me a lot." He shook his head slightly. "He was good for me and my mom, incredibly supportive. He's the reason I didn't end up in juvenile detention, which would've destroyed my chances at public service."

"Sounds like a good man."

"Yeah, he is. But don't tell him I said that."

They pulled into Elliott's and parked. The man walked up and down the aisles with purpose, knowing just what he was looking for and where to find it. Maybe all hardware stores were set up the same way because in record time, he had everything he needed, and they were checking out.

Driving back onto church property, Lynée asked, "So how much longer do you want to work?" She didn't know if staying here watching him work shirtless was the best of ideas. He'd probably ruin not only her mental functioning but her executive functioning as well.

He glanced at his watch. "Not sure."

"How about I leave you here to finish, and I'll head over to Skye's house and water her plants, bring in the mail, all that stuff."

He looked her way. "All right. But I should probably shower afterward." His lips pinched to the side like he was formulating a plan. "I'll shower at the motel, then we can go out for dinner. Sound good?"

That meant she would wait in his motel room while he showered. She turned her head at a car passing by. She couldn't think of any logical reason that wouldn't be okay. She swallowed hard. "All right. Sounds good to me. Call me when you're finished. I'll pick you up."

He nodded and, with the bag in hand, headed for the back of the church.

Jace in a shower. The view of him without a shirt and

cutting lumber was one heck of tongue-swallow. But imagining his back glistening with beads of water in a stall-full of steam...His tattoos in clear view as he combed his hair at the vanity.

Tattoos weren't for her, but it certainly seemed to suit him. And the artwork itself was exquisite. Beauty on the beast.

Somehow she shook herself from that momentary trance and drove off toward her friend's house.

Lynnie, don't think about being close to this man. Think about helping Skye. Finish the work, Skye can come home, and Jace will leave.

That last thought left her more unsettled then thinking about the man being naked on the other side of a wall.

Didn't matter. He would finish his work and leave, and that's that.

***

Jace set the box of wood screws on the workbench in the shed.

Fr Richard walked in, carrying cold bottles of water. "Can I get you anything else?"

"No, thanks. I'm good."

He stretched the ruler and drew markings on the side and back pieces of the bookshelf. Focusing extra hard on the task in front of him, and not the wild thoughts tormenting his mind.

Lynée leaving him here was a blessing in disguise. That stunned and hungry look in her eyes when she saw him shirtless... He'd seen that look before on other women and had never given it much credence. But with Lynée, it was an entirely different experience. She looked like she could eat him up in one damn bite, and he *wanted* it.

It took everything he had not to look at her in the car or in the hardware store. If he did, he'd probably have taken her right then.

Visions of her, alone in the shed, and all the incredible things his dirty imagination craved made him so uncomfortable in his pants.

Turning to grab the drill, he discreetly adjusted himself.

"I'll hold this here," Fr Richard said as he squatted down, holding the shelf against the side plank.

God was taunting him. He shouldn't be thinking about all the delicious things he wanted to do to Lynée while on church property. That was highly inappropriate. Talk about temptation. Any second, he expected lightning to strike him down. How many Hail Mary's would it take to prevent that?

Shit! He sounded like Lynée. He chuckled to himself.

He couldn't say why he wanted to build this damn bookshelf. It probably had everything to do with the look on Lynée's face when she saw that children's book trashed. She must have known that book. Probably had it read to her a million times.

Jace couldn't relate to being connected to a book that much, but he could certainly relate to that look on her face. It was the same expression his mother gave when he was a teenager and had thrown his father's cross in the trash. That heartbroken expression that he absolutely refused to let another woman experience, not if he could help it.

Their case would just have to wait. They could make up the lost time tomorrow. Hopefully, this wouldn't take but another day, and the church could put their library back together.

Lining up the shelf, the screws drilled through the wood like butter.

Jace only had four shelves done when his phone rang. *Lynée.*

CHAPTER 19

THE WOMAN'S CAR sat parked in the short driveway. But from the last hour of watching her place a few houses down, Emilio was certain Skye Winters wasn't home. Judging from the mail overflowing her mailbox, she'd probably gone hiding with Monroe somewhere.

He pulled up his hoodie and started toward her house. With a quick vault over her back fence, he made his way to the back door. The lock picked easily enough, but he turned the knob, and it didn't budge.

The deadbolt.

Emilio rolled his eyes. With his fist balled into his sleeve, he punched out the window on the door, then reached around to undo the deadbolt. Inside, the smell of apple permeated the air. The two dark beams stretching across the vaulted ceilings into a living area made the small space seem bigger than it was. The woman was a fan of fresh plants but clearly hadn't been home in a while. Some were starting to wilt. Framed photos lined most of the walls, painted cheerful colors. But none of the pictures included Monroe.

After searching her kitchen, sifting through multiple junk drawers and the mail on her counter, he didn't find many clues to Monroe's whereabouts. Or any details about him at all. The fridge was full of rabbit food, vitamin waters, and apple jelly. The leftover dish of what looked like lasagna looked pretty good. The freezer was a disappointment as well. A basket full of apples sat on the other counter.

There's got to be something here.

Lots of photographs of her and her parents were displayed around the house, as well as several with her and another blonde woman in glasses. Skye had left her laptop sitting on the counter, her screensaver more images of her and this other woman. The thing was password-protected, so he couldn't get in. He wasn't tech-savvy like Monroe or Diego.

Damn, this woman was starting to annoy him. He grabbed the lightweight computer, yanking the power cord from the wall and smashed it on the floor.

In her bedroom, a bright light flooded in through the windows across the unmade bed. Her open closet appeared messy with overturned hangars and a few garments on the floor, as though she'd packed some things quickly. Rifling through her dresser drawers revealed she had an affinity for lacy underwear. But nothing from or about a boyfriend.

The man didn't keep any clothes or belongings here.

What woman doesn't have pictures of her boyfriend in her bedroom?

He searched through her bathroom. Not even a toothbrush.

A faint clicking noise made him stop.

The front door opened, and the soft sound of a woman's voice followed. "So much mail."

Emilio grinned. Skye must've returned home. Maybe Monroe was with her. He placed a hand over the handle of his gun tucked in his waistband. He'd wait back here patiently, ready to pounce.

"Holy mother of cheese and rice!" she called.

She must have just noticed the kitchen with the smashed laptop, open cabinet doors, and the open fridge. He looked in the bathroom mirror, through the reflection of the partially open door. The woman's small frame stood mostly blocked by a wall. He couldn't see her face, but the hair was a little darker than in the pictures. No one else came in behind her.

She was alone.

He bit back a growl. At least now, he was one very large step closer to his target. She must know where he'd run to. All he had to do was torture the information out of her.

"Oh no," she muttered, still oblivious to his presence. "This is the last thing she needs." The lady pulled out a cell phone and pressed a few buttons. "Jace, it's Lynée. Skye's house has been broken into."

Emilio seethed. It wasn't her.

Mierda!

After a short pause, she continued. "I don't know how they got in, the front door was still locked. Oh wait... The glass from the back door is broken. Probably just some rowdy teenagers. Can you ask Fr. Richard to bring you over? I'll call the sheriff as well. I need to start cleaning up this mess."

Now Emilio would have to kill another person just to escape unseen. He double-checked the clip inside his gun. As soon as she drew closer to the bathroom, he'd plug one in her head.

She moved back through the house, closer to where he hid behind the door. "Oh, that's a good idea," she continued into the phone. "Her insurance will need pictures of the damage, too. Can I please call Skye and let her know what's going on?"

He stopped. This woman knew where Skye was. Maybe Monroe was with her, too.

Que chingon! Adrenaline pulsed through his veins. In only a matter of hours, he could dance his way to the prick's doorstep and have a tequila shot over the man's body.

Lynée sighed. "Fine. Do everything yourself, as usual. Just get over here." She reminded him of the address and hung up.

The girl's face was soft and angelic. Her glasses made her bright green eyes bigger. She was so close, just an arm's length away now. He tightened his grip on the gun, ready to grab her. He held his breath.

She turned away and went back to the living room. Then she held up her phone and shot several pictures, turning in slow circles, getting every inch of the room.

Maybe if he just followed her around for a little while, she'd lead him straight to his targets. She didn't even have to know. Catching Monroe and his girlfriend by surprise heightened his chances of success. Granted, his boss was growing impatient, but surely a day or two would bring him right to the DEA agent's doorstep.

Now, to get out unseen. She was busy snapping pictures. It would be so easy to grab her, drag her into his car, and have some fun with her. Maybe after...

***

A small thump from the back of the house pulled Lynée's attention around. She hadn't even imagined the robbers still being in the house. Jace had told her not to touch anything, in fact, to go to her car to wait for him. But that was ridiculous. He was so paranoid. Occupational hazard, probably.

"Hello?" she called.

No response.

She slowly moved to the back bedroom. All of the dresser drawers were open, and Skye's clothes thrown about. Including some bras and underwear. *Creepy suckers.* She moved farther down the hallway to the bathroom. Everything remained untouched. Except her shower curtain was pulled closed. An image of a dozen horror movies flashed in her mind of a serial killer hiding behind the clichéd shower curtain.

She grabbed the plunger from beside the toilet and used it to quickly draw back the curtain. Empty.

With a shake of her head, Lynée chided herself. "That man's fixations are messing with my head."

She looked to her left—the bathroom window was wide open. Her breath caught. Boosting up on the toilet, she stuck her head out and inspected the back patio.

No one was there. Nothing seemed out of place either.

She closed the window and locked it.

As she finished her first pass-through of Skye's house, nothing seemed missing. Strange, they didn't just steal her laptop. Instead, they shattered it. All her other electronics were left untouched as well.

"What were they looking for?" she asked herself.

She grabbed the dustpan and brush from the closet and went to work on cleaning up the broken glass at the back door. This was going to take a long time to clean up, with tiny fragments stuck in the grout. She nearly groaned. No matter how many times she'd run the vacuum or a mop, it would never be completely clean again.

"Lynée?" a distant voice called from the front door.

She turned to see Jace bounding up the front porch steps with a touch of panic in his face. He drew his weapon from his holster.

"I'm in here. Nothing looks stolen."

The sheriff's vehicle pulled up to the curb just as Jace reached her side. "I told you to wait outside."

"They broke in through the back door, destroyed Skye's laptop and rummaged through things, but didn't take anything. Who does that?"

"Someone looking for her. To get to Monroe. Someone like the cartel." He started moving through the rooms, his weapon up, clearing the house.

"No one is here. I've already looked."

The sheriff walked in, his own weapon drawn as well. "Miss Clark?" His eyes were shadowed by his wide-brimmed hat.

"Afternoon, Wyatt. I'm so sorry to trouble you with this."

"It's my job. May I ask you to step outside while I clear the house?"

"Already clear," Jace called from the back. He walked up the hallway and re-holstered his pistol. He nodded to Wyatt. "Afternoon, Sheriff."

"This town was super quiet for a long time, and as soon as you roll in, all hell keeps breaking loose." He frowned. The man's bushy gray eyebrows matched his uniform.

"In more ways than one," Lynée muttered under her breath and pulled up her phone to scan through the photos.

"Well, it's a stupid question since I already know the answer, but do either of you have any idea who would've done this?" His long sigh signaled his fatigue as he pulled out his notepad.

"Considering the perpetrators didn't steal anything," Jace answered, "more than likely, this is related to the former DEA agent in my custody."

The two lawmen continued discussing things while she

kept scrolling through her photos. Skye was going to be pissed when she saw her shattered laptop. But not as mad when she realized someone had gone through her bedroom drawers. Hopefully, Jace would finally let her talk to her best friend. Granted, she'd only be giving her more bad news, but she so longed to hear her voice. She'd soften it with the good news that all her plants were still alive.

"I'll board up her back window real quick, then we should go." Jace came up behind her. "Did you get pictures of everything? I need to include it in my investigation files."

"Yeah, I think so." She scrolled through a few more photos.

"Wait, stop!" he barked.

She jumped.

"Go back." He brushed a large arm over her shoulder and skimmed his finger across the screen to the shot of the hallway. "Zoom in on the bathroom."

Lynée enlarged the photo and focused on the slightly open door. Then gasped.

A tiny reflection in the mirror, behind the partially open door, was the distinct face of a man. A Hispanic, leathery-skinned face with a scruffy chin glared hungrily at her.

All words left her mind. She couldn't even think. The guy had been there the whole time.

Wait, she'd checked the bathroom, the stupid maneuver with the plunger. It was empty. When had he...

"Sheriff!" Jace barked out the front door. "We have a suspect."

Her hands shook, the full realization just now hitting her. The guy could've attacked her. Shot her or sliced her throat. Or he could've grabbed her, dragged her out the back door, and been long gone before Jace arrived. She'd been inches away from never being seen again. Inches away from death.

Why didn't he attack?

"We'll put this through facial recognition software and see if we can identify him." Jace took her phone from her hands, and shared the image with Wyatt, nearly salivating at this new piece of evidence. "Can you run it through your database as well? Just to make sure he isn't a local."

"No one I recognize," he answered gruffly. "But, we can put out a BOLO."

"No. I don't want him to see we have his picture. That'll make him run. But I need a name."

Lynée walked out the front door, needing fresh air. The two men kept talking inside, but all she could focus on was the danger surrounding her best friend. This man was after Skye, to get to Reed. Just as Jace predicted.

Down each end of the street, she didn't see anyone else. No cars, no dog walkers— nothing. In the middle of the afternoon, everyone would be at work. Where had that man disappeared to? He'd vanished into the cold, dry air. Or perhaps he ducked behind a tree somewhere. Was he watching her right now? Smiling to himself, thinking he'd gotten away with it?

She ground her teeth and took another deep breath. "You won't get away with this," she muttered to void. "We're going to stop you."

For Skye.

CHAPTER 20

JACE ROLLED UP to Lynée's house the next morning, the motorcycle engine echoing down the street. The air turned chillier overnight, and the news forecasted snow later that day. Nothing that would accumulate, but definitely signaling an early winter. He switched off the engine and studied the front of her house.

What if it had been Lynée these cartel thugs were after? What if he weren't here to help her? But that was part of the job. He wouldn't always be here. He'd have to go chase down leads and suspects. She would be left alone. A lot.

He had to finish this. Fast.

The two of them had buried themselves in mountains of evidence and files for days, and he still didn't feel any closer to closing this thing. If it hadn't been for Lynée, this whole process would've taken infinitely longer. With his suspect hiding out in protective custody, and this cartel assassin on his ass, they didn't have infinite time.

He strolled up her walkway and took a deep breath before knocking. He checked the doorknob. Locked.

Good. She'd finally learned something from him.

She opened the door, her glasses perched on the edge of her nose. She still wore her flannel pajama pants and an oversized sweater. So cozy looking, all he wanted to do was curl up with her on the couch.

"Mornin'. Just made a fresh pot of coffee."

"Thanks." He closed the door behind him.

Her green eyes read eager and determined. "Jace, I need to call Skye. We have to tell her what happened."

"I agree." He pulled the phone from his back pocket, called the number, and handed it to her. "Give it back when you're done so I can talk to Reed."

She nodded and took the phone, greedily listening for a pickup. "Reed, it's Lynée. Can I talk to Skye?"

Her friend got on the line, her voice loud enough for him to overhear. "Lynnie, is everything okay?"

"Not exactly. We're fine, but... someone broke into your house yesterday." She recounted the events from the burglary, including her broken backdoor and smashed laptop.

Jace moved a little closer and heard Skye's expletive through the phone.

"It's just a laptop, easy to replace. The good news is Sheriff Wyatt and the DEA have the guy's picture from...surveillance, to see if they can find anything... Yes, I promise. I'll call and get some bids to replace the door glass."

Jace was grateful Lynée didn't go into an explanation over where the picture came from. The last thing they wanted to do was scare the crap out of them. He waved his fingers, needing the phone back to make sure she didn't give them more than they needed to know.

"I gotta hand the phone to Jace. Put Reed on, okay?"

He took the cell. "Look, Monroe, they're gonna run the picture through the database—"

"It's the cartel." Monroe's voice was curt...adamant.

Jace nodded as if the guy could see him. "Likely. I'll

text you his picture, let me know if you recognize him." He hit a few buttons on the phone and waited for a response.

"No. But he found our trail pretty damn fast."

"I know. Just hang tight. Make sure you don't leave that house. We'll get these bastards."

"Keep me posted."

"I will," and he disconnected the call. He slipped the phone in his back pocket and gripped the edge of the stair banister. The more he thought about it, the more he really didn't like this.

"What?" Her eyebrows pinched together.

"I don't want you staying here by yourself."

Her smirk was almost as adorable as her smile. "Don't start that."

"Just for a few days until they find him."

"I don't need a babysitter. I've lived just fine on my own for years."

"You haven't had a cartel hitman on your tail before. I need to make sure you stay safe. My first suggestion is I stay here, but I know how small towns are. Your reputation and everything…"

She cocked her head and put her hands on her hips. Just the way Tinkerbell did in Peter Pan. So stubborn and adorable. "How noble."

"I mean it, Lynée. I'm not being cute or sarcastic. You need protection right now."

"No, thanks." She turned back around to the box of evidence.

He nearly growled. She was so damn frustrating. "You don't get a choice. I'll call the sheriff. Request he put a man in front of your house overnight."

"I'm positive Wyatt, and his deputies have better things to do than sit out in the cold all night long." She ran her fingers through her hair and shook out the tangles. "Besides, that's the best way to ensure all the gossip about my reputation makes the complete circuit around town...a cop car sitting outside my house for days."

"Not days. Just overnights. I'll be here during the day."

With a flip of her hair, she gave him an incredulous look. "All day every day? What happens if you need to run out and get lunch? Or go do your agent things and run down a lead? Good heavens, how will I ever manage on my own if you have to go to the bathroom?"

He closed the distance between them in two large strides. "You know what? This is how." He pulled his cell phone out of his pocket and called Sheriff Wyatt. After a brief conversation, the man agreed to help provide protection, and in fact, was happy to send a deputy over right then. Jace ended the call.

Lynée glared. "Why in the world does he have to come over now? You've completely let your power run amuck in your head."

"I told you, you're not gonna be left alone for the near future." He turned and grabbed his keys off the coffee table. "And, I need some air." He stood by the front door, waiting for the police car to pull up.

She followed with her hands on her hips. "You've been in a pissy mood ever since you walked through that door. What stick crawled up your behind?"

He chuckled, only because her attempts at cursing and sounding vulgar sounded like a toddler. But she wasn't wrong. He had been in a *pissy* mood. Not just because she was infuriating and stubborn and countering everything he'd said. But because he was angry with himself. For not having better control over this case, and letting a maniac get this close to her. Hell, the woman had only been inches away from unthinkable torture, and here she was arguing with him about having a little extra protection.

"Don't ignore me," she warned. "Is that what you do when someone disagrees with you? You run off so you don't have to hear it. You see, that's the problem with people today. They are completely incapable of handling discord in a mature, productive manner. Let me guess, in whatever law enforcement academy you attended, you were taught to bulldoze people for having differing opinions and find the closest exit with the path of least resistance."

He rolled his eyes skyward and forced a deep breath before he responded. "No, Lynée. I was taught to arrest people. To completely ignore whatever bullshit stories they concocted to get out of being slapped in handcuffs. Then I was taught to defend myself against physical altereations so they wouldn't pose a danger to the rest of society. To innocent civilians like *you*."

By some miracle, the deputy's car pulled up in front of her house right then.

"Hallelujah." He threw open the door and tossed one instruction over his shoulder. "Make sure you lock this door."

With a few quick instructions to the officer and exchanging contact info, he threw a leg over his Harley and drove off.

CHAPTER 21

JACE NEEDED TO think. And he could always think better on his bike. He took off through the mountains, breathing in the fresh air, taking in the change of scenery. Thinking about the break-in at Skye's house and the image of that son of a bitch in the bathroom mirror. His mind should've been focused on the case and finding out who that man was, how he was connected with the cartel, and finding an end to this whole mess. Because he was certain it was all connected. Hell, he could easily see how that was the same man in the car on the surveillance video from the motel explosion.

But all he could think about was how damn close Lynée had come to being killed. That bastard could've jumped her at any moment. And Jace would've been too late to stop it. His vivid imagination afflicted him with the images of previous gruesome crime scenes, any one of them could've happened to her.

The cold air slapped his face going down the mountain. This was why he'd remained unattached in his career. These thoughts drove men insane. Drove damn-good agents to desk jobs and early retirement because they were worried about significant others. That something would happen to them. Or to themselves, leaving their significant others to mourn in agony.

His mother suffered horribly after his father's death. He'd seen her sob on the bathroom floor countless times, and she had stayed in bed all day for months on end. He'd vowed to himself to never do that to a woman in his life. The only way to ensure that was to never let one get close.

Dammit, Lynée was getting too close. Or more specifically, he was allowing himself to get too close to her. What was more, he couldn't bring himself to back off. Not even a little. With that break-in and her unknowingly near-miss with death, he wanted to hold on tighter. Make *sure* she stayed safe. Beside him.

He drove for a while when his stomach started talking to him. *Time to feed the beast.*

Scoping out the town, he found a cafe to eat his usual—a sandwich with extra meat, soup, chips, pasta salad, and a tall glass of milk. Just as he dug into the food, his phone buzzed.

Caller ID showed it was Phil.

"Hey, old-timer," he answered.

"Just checkin' on you." Phil's voice sounded raspier than usual, but still upbeat. "How's your case coming?"

"It's been...interesting."

"I would imagine so. It's not every day you investigate a crooked DEA agent. Is he still under wraps right now?"

Jace paused with his fork dangling over his plate. "Why?"

"I heard there's a cartel assassin in your neck of the woods. Is that related to your guy?"

Absolutely. "Might be. You saw the notice we put out?"

"Everyone has. And based on our last conversation, that's why I wanted to make sure you're okay. Do you need any kind of backup?"

"No, I have it under control. I have someone helping me look through all the data."

"Really? Who?"

"A local." He wasn't quite ready to share with him this local was a woman, a librarian, who'd spent most of his days with.

The background noise silenced as if Phil had stepped into a different room or closed his office door for privacy. "Look, I remember these guys from my field days. They're not amateurs. So whatever you're doing on your case, you need to wrap it up ASAP. I understand if you're not comfortable bringing in someone from the El Paso office to help you. But I can send someone I trust. You just need to tell me where."

He sat back in his chair. "You know I can't do that."

"I would never ask you to betray your gut. If this guy is truly being framed by another crooked agent, we owe it to him to help him out of this. But more importantly, I need to make sure you're safe."

"I appreciate that, Phil. But I can handle myself."

"I mean it, J. I don't like what I'm hearing coming up the chain. You need to be careful."

He raised his eyes skyward. "I will, Mom."

"Don't be an ass," he snapped, "or I *will* call your mother. How much longer do you need?"

"Not sure. We're close, though."

"We? You mean the local? What kind of qualifications do they have?"

"I'm...not comfortable sharing that right now." He looked around him, with several other patrons sitting a little too close to overhear.

"Fine. Let me know when you're finished. If *anything*

goes haywire, you call me."

"I will. Take care."

He finished his meal, realizing it had been far too long since he'd last seen his mentor. Even longer since he'd sat down to dinner with both Phil and his mom. Maybe over Christmas, they could all get back together again.

As he strode back to his bike, a store caught his eye—a butcher.

Steak.

Damn. When was the last time he had a really thick juicy steak? The diner doesn't count. His stomach turned over. He left his bike and strolled inside.

If Lynée didn't have a grill, he could easily cook the steaks in a skillet with butter. Not as tasty as from a grill, but it would do the job. He could practically smell the juicy, tender prime beef. This time he'd make sure there wasn't a single ketchup bottle in sight.

Maybe he could use this as an olive branch. She'd been right. He was angry and ended up taking it out on her.

When he arrived, the deputy's car still sat by the curb. The man had a plate of muffins and a thermos of some hot liquid. No doubt Lynée had provided those treats, probably meant as an apology.

Once inside, he spotted her staring at a wall of pictures, her glasses sliding down her nose, and a pen tucked behind her ear. She'd changed into a loose button-down blouse, steel-blue, and a gray wool skirt that reached her knees. Still very academic, but with a little more leg than she usually showed. The look was quite becoming. A little furrow in her brow proved she'd been thinking too hard.

The other wall was covered with more papers. The corkboard from the church was in the center, with dozens of different color strings keeping track of various events in a long timeline.

"Holy shit, woman."

She tapped her pen on a few photos in front of her. "Don't touch my system over there. It's all coded."

"Care to explain it to me?" Maybe they could call a truce over work.

She turned around, her skirt furling a bit in the twirl, and she stared at her creation. "Green and teal strings are the financials, DEA events in red, news articles about the cartel in purple, Reed's files in yellow, the black are Joe's reports..." She continued on with the various categories. "I was trying to see where various lines crossed."

Her research mode was in full throttle, and it was as intimidating as hell. He glanced at the far wall with all the photos.

"What is this stuff, Bell?" He set the bags on the counter.

"Cabello family tree."

He nearly snorted and came up beside her. There had been countless agents working on that cartel affiliation over the years, probably all staring at the same thing. But he wouldn't disrupt her line of thinking.

"What did you find?"

"Lots and lots of dead relatives."

"A testament to the cartel lifestyle." He recognized Carlos Cabello at the top, as well as a few others taped to the wall, all connected by various colored strings. Diego Huerta's picture was off to the side, unconnected.

"As I come across an incident in Reed's reports—a contact or a suspect—I print off a picture and stick it on the wall. Then I research them to see how they're connected."

"Damn." He put his hands on his hips, stunned by the sheer number of people she'd uncovered from the reports.

And had found their photos.

"If this wasn't a visual-enough tale to convince people *not* to go into the drug trade," she continued, "then nothing would." She bit her lip in that adorable way and stepped forward to point at some pictures. "Carlos had a dozen brothers and sisters, of whom half died during childhood. The other half became grunt workers for the cartel, especially the women's husbands. A bunch of children from those siblings, many of whom ended up killed in one capacity or another. This brother here," she pointed to a more sadistic looking man that was clearly copied from an old newspaper clipping. "He was one of Carlos' key enforcers for years before a heart attack at age forty-one. Never married, but a bunch of newspaper articles refer to several illegitimate children, who were raised on the Cabello compound. Which, according to a watchdog reporter, is also heavily protected by the local police. Carlos, on the other hand, has never been married and doesn't appear to have any kids. Really strange, considering everyone else has or had at least five."

He loved the determination in her voice, that unwavering focus. "Okay, so where are you stuck?"

"This guy." She pointed to Diego Huerta's photo. "I'm trying to figure out how he fits in."

"Monroe said he was the computer genius. And a bounty notice for Reed Monroe claimed for the death of Carlos's nephew. Can we assume Huerta was the nephew?"

"A nephew..." she thought out loud. "From which sibling?" She sifted through a file and pulled out a paper. "His birth certificate lists the mother's name, but no father. Mom isn't related to the Cabello family at all. But her death certificate is only a few years later," she pulled another paper, "under suspicious circumstances. I can't find her picture."

"What do you mean, suspicious circumstances?"

"The cause of death was crossed out. And it says *un asunto familiar*. I translated it to 'a family matter.'"

"Okay. As amazing as this family tree is, and your level of detail is exceptional, why is this important?"

She gave him an incredulous look. "Reed's reports and files are thorough. They list names and contact info for everyone, and each specific date Joe interacted with them. And everyone is coming back as a family member. Very few outsiders. Everything this guy does involves family. They're all interconnected somewhere." Her eyes narrowed, looking at the data.

"Which means..."

Lynée sighed. "If you want to capture Carlos Cabello, DEA needs to track and follow his family members."

"True. But we're not here to do that. We're here to see if Monroe is telling the truth. Was he the mole, or his former partner, Joe?"

"That's what I'm saying. There is no connection between Reed and Cabello. None. But Joe, on the other hand..." She bit her lip again and turned away from the wall. She stood in front of a different box.

"What? You're saying there's a connection?"

"I'm not sure." She pulled out a file. "I hated doing this because I know Reed thought so highly of him. But Joe had several cousins and siblings who went to prison for drugs. Including one for distribution."

"That doesn't mean they're connected to the Cabellos."

"True. But they all lived in El Paso. And what if the cartel got to Joe through *his* family? They knew Joe was DEA and needed an insider. So if his relative was running drugs for the Cabellos and realized they could threaten Joe into working for them or his family member would be killed... Do you think he'd do it?"

Jace chewed on this inside of his cheek. "I'd like to say no, but it isn't the first time they've gotten to an agent that way."

"So it's more likely that Joe was the mole and not Reed."

"More likely, yes. But that's not enough to clear him of these charges. We need definitive proof."

She clumped down into the loveseat and pulled her glasses off. Then she rubbed her eyes. "Proof that Joe was the mole."

"Joe, or anyone else. Though, since Joe was the one who first alerted the existence of a mole, that's unlikely as well." He knelt in front of her, caressing her thighs over the wool. "Listen, you've done exemplary work here. I can imagine the amount of time and effort involved in this eye-crossing computer work. You would make one hell of an analyst."

The side of her mouth quirked up at him, her face still defeated as she plucked at her skirt's hem. She'd tried so hard to help exonerate her friend. So she and Monroe could come home.

"Don't give up. We follow the evidence, no matter where it leads."

"I know I'm right, Jace. I can't prove it yet. But you'll see."

His heart sank. "I hope so."

"You don't sound like it."

"I'm thinking about where the case goes if Reed is found innocent."

"Meaning?"

"The mole is still out there...and both of them are still

not safe."

A flash of worry crossed her face.

He loved the way she was an open book. How every emotion played on her face each moment. For a librarian, the cliché was heartwarming.

"Then we'll do it. We'll figure it out. And they can come home." He exhaled. "Look, Lynée, about earlier—"

She met his gaze. "It's all right. I know you're just trying to protect me. For that, I'm grateful."

The corners of his lips curved slightly. He was thankful they didn't need to speak about it anymore. At least one thing went right that day. He held out his hand.

She slipped her fingers in it, squeezing him back.

"Okay, now that that's clear," he stood and helped her to her feet, "let me show you what I bought us for dinner."

CHAPTER 22

"OH MY GOSH, Jace." Lynée leaned back in her chair and exhaled. "That dinner was perfection. I can't tell you the last time I had steak."

"Perfection?"

She licked her lips. "Don't let it go to your head."

He lifted a brow.

Why did it seem everything had a sexual connotation with this man? She huffed and rose to take her plate to the kitchen.

This man filled her thoughts way too much, and not because of work. How did she rein in these crazy images? For the first time ever, she even had a naughty dream about him—his confident smile and sculpted cheekbones. Just remembering it brought heat to her cheeks. She shook her head and reached up to put away the pepper grinder.

Suddenly, he was there.

She froze.

"Lynée, despite what you think, remember that I am perfection."

"You're cocky, that's what you are." She choked out, trying to keep it playful, but still unable to turn around.

His beard tickled the side of her neck as he stroked her hair to one side, leaving a trail of tingles over her skin. "That

I am." His manhood pressed against her backside.

She inhaled sharply. Oh God. When was the last time she was with a man? Years of celibacy left her clearly sexually frustrated, to the point she considered being with this brute of a man.

He placed a small kiss on her neck, then another. "I could touch you, Bell. Show you what you've been missing." His hand slid up the side of her thigh.

Oh yes! She loved what he did to her.

Wait. No! Absolutely not.

Her eyes flew open. "I don't think that's a good idea, Jace."

He kissed her neck more, traveling toward the back as he pushed her hair higher to expose more skin. "You're right, it's not a good idea. It's a great idea."

"No means no, Jace."

"It absolutely does."

More kisses brought her to nearly panting.

She was acutely aware of a pressure building in her lower belly. She shifted her legs closer together.

"But you didn't tell me 'no.'" His hand lifted her skirt to caress the bare skin on her thigh. "If you tell me no, I'll stop this very second. Or you simply stand there and let my fingers roam parts of your body that are dying for attention."

Holy cannoli! They certainly are.

His hand glossed over the edge of her cotton panties at her hip. Teasing her. Tantalizing her.

Her lady-parts ached like she never knew before. Her face grew warm just thinking about what his fingers could do if they'd only move over a few more inches.

He slid the tip of his tongue along her neck and back down again. "But I'll need your help."

She could barely think. His tongue had taken away all her brain cells. "My help?"

"Lift your skirt, and I'll slide your panties down these beautiful legs."

Her mouth turned instantly dry. The words wouldn't come.

"Can you do that, Bell?"

Could she? Could she give in to this man? Let him touch her in an intimate and oh-so-delicious way? They weren't married. They weren't even dating. She'd never considered anything so scandalous.

But crap-on-a-cracker, his hands felt so darn good.

Her fingers came to the wool garment, slowly gathering the fabric in her hands. Cool air graced her warm skin.

"A little higher," he whispered into her ear.

She pulled her skirt over her bottom, her undies completely visible.

"That's perfect, Bell." His large warm hands glided over both globes, massaging and kneading the flesh.

She moaned as her head fell forward, her glasses sliding to the tip of her nose.

His fingertips hooked under the waistband of her panties and drew them down. Slowly, deliberately drawn out, probably to see if she'd protest.

Oh my. The lower half of her body was completely naked. This man could see everything.

"Step out, Bell."

She did as he bid and waited for more. She couldn't believe this was happening, but she was too eager for more. The moisture at her sex felt cool in the open air.

"Bell, you have the most beautiful ass." He placed a kiss on each cheek and stood. His hands returned to caressing her bare bottom. "Spread your legs a little for me."

She complied, her knees a little shaky, and his fingers quickly found her center.

She inhaled suddenly as his fingers slid over her nether lips and through her center.

"Christ, you're wet." He gently kicked her legs farther apart and pushed against her back, bending her at the waist. His finger grazed over her clitoris.

A surge of heat pulsed in that tiny spot. "Mm," she moaned and placed her hands on the counter to keep steady.

"My sweet Bell, I don't think this will take long." He caressed and circled her hot button, over and over.

The pulsing increased in intensity, and the heat oh so thrilling. She couldn't help herself from swaying forward and back in time with his finger, before he pushed a whole digit inside her.

"How is this?" he hummed into her ear. "Does this feel good?"

"More, please," she whispered.

He repeated his ministrations, now adding a second finger. "Whatever the lady wants." He pumped his fingers into her while his thumb massaged her clit.

The most-delightful sensations built from deep inside her. The only sounds were her little sighs of pleasure and panting, and his breath on her neck. The sensations coiled together so tightly right over her clitoris, threatening to release any second. In all her time with her marriage, it had never been like this. So intense and so quick. Finally, the coil sprang loose, and her climax exploded. She screamed out, riding that uncontrollable and irresistible wave.

He didn't stop until her knees buckled and she collapsed on the counter.

She was aware of her skirt carefully being shimmied back into place. He helped steady her upright. With heavy lids, she opened her eyes and turned her head to face him.

He slipped his two fingers into his mouth, all the way to the knuckles, and slowly drew them out, licking every inch. "Delicious."

She gasped.

He slipped off her glasses, setting them on the counter. Then he leaned closer, his lips inches from hers. "Did you enjoy that?"

Words failed her, so she nodded.

"I promised you would." He scanned her face one last time before he crashed his lips onto hers. She let his ravenous tongue enter her mouth and roam freely. She dared herself to dance her own tongue with his. She mewled at the sensations and flavors of this strong man dominating her mouth, his whiskers tingling her skin.

Their kiss deepened for several long moments, and his body pressed against hers. His thick erection dug into her belly, so rigid and strong, until he broke away. His eyes darkened as he gazed into hers. "The next time I see you, I'm doing that again, only it will be with my mouth."

She held her breath, hardly able to process what he just said.

Was he serious?

The thought made her sex muscles tighten.

Before she could protest, inform him this was only a one-time show from a simple moment of weakness, he spun around and headed for the door.

Jacket and helmet in hand, he called back to her, "Lock up behind me." He winked and pulled the door closed.

Her shaky breath matched her wobbly legs as they carried her to the front door, turning the deadbolt. She pivoted and leaned against the door, then let gravity carry her body slowly down to the ground.

Oh, my goodness.

What was that? Did he just do that to me? Did I just let him?

They were working together. This was not appropriate.

Her hands cradled her hot cheeks. The man had sworn he'd do it again. And she desperately wanted him to.

Oh, dear Lord. I'm in big trouble.

His hard-on raged against his pants. He never wanted to be inside a woman as badly as with Lynée. But she was not his type, not even close. His type wore low-cut shirts, ample cleavage, short, tight skirts, extra makeup including lipstick that would smear all over his rock-hard dick.

Lynée was an innocent. Of course, that didn't change the fact that he wanted to fuck the sensibilities right out of her.

The second he walked through his motel room door, he stripped out of his clothes, dropping his shit anywhere. He flipped on the shower and stepped in when it was barely hot enough.

Fuck! He took himself in hand. His erection had grown painful, he needed relief quickly. That vixen brought out the worst in him. Or the best, depending on the perspective.

He couldn't be playing with her like that. He knew better. A woman like that deserves a man who could commit, one willing to devote the rest of his life to her. The picket fence, two-and-a-half kids, and Sunday brunches. Jace was not that man.

So why couldn't he keep his hands off her? Why such low self-control?

He'd been on cases that had tried his patience, but he

never caved. He could wait it out with the best of them. He knew the first person to flinch loses.

Well, this wasn't some kind of stake-out, but the rules still applied. Patience was warranted. Work the case, not the woman. The only reason the two of them were even together was that she wanted to help her friend. She didn't even like him.

But she was gorgeous. Those adorable Tinkerbell lips drove him mad, and the second he laid eyes on that ample bosom, he was lost. The way she opened for him just now...so wet...so wanting.

"Fuck," he exhaled on his release.

As he toweled off, he stared at the reflection in the mirror. He shouldn't have told her he'd do more too. He couldn't fucking stop himself. He wanted to make her feel good, to watch her scream out the best orgasm she'd ever had. He wanted her hot and eager for what he could give her. To feel firsthand what it was like to have a man appreciate a body like hers, to worship her the way she should be.

"Yes, but that didn't mean you were supposed to be that guy." He shook his head in disgust. He vowed to keep his hands to himself when it came to Lynée. Work only. Solve this damn case.

CHAPTER 23

EMILIO WATCHED THIS blonde woman's house from down the block, his ass starting to grow numb from hours of sitting. He'd managed to follow her home unseen after breaking into Skye Winters' home. A mountainous man was glued to her side the whole time. From the way that *cabron* walked and surveyed everything, he was definitely law enforcement.

Now police cars sat outside her house.

Which were both huge *chupacabras* circling the fiesta.

But this woman was the key. The key to finding Skye and Monroe. She had to know where they were hiding, or when they'd be back. He'd follow her as much as he could without getting caught to find out her routine. When she was alone, he would strike. It only took patience.

His cell phone buzzed in his pocket. He already knew it was his boss and answered on the first ring. "*Si, jefe.*"

"You better have good news for me." Cabello's voice sounded furious. Still calm, but low and stinging. Like a rattlesnake, ready to strike. Which meant something had gone wrong.

"I'm much closer. I found the best friend. I'll make her sing like a mockingbird, and give up their location."

"Good. You need to hurry. DEA has your face blasted

on all their screens. You were made."

Que chingados! Emilio twisted his grip on the steering wheel, the leather creaking from the pressure. *How the hell did they get my picture?*

"You're much smarter than that, E." The cartel boss' voice shook with rage. "Tell me you're not getting sloppy with this dangling carrot of a bounty. Or are you growing incompetent in your old age?"

"Of course not, *señor*. I'll wrap this up in a fucking ribbon for you, and be home by the weekend. With your present in the trunk."

"*Bueno*. Do it now. You're out of time."

***

Lynée awoke to her phone, dinging with a text. She lifted the screen to see it was from Jace.

Heading to the gym this morning. Then I'll bring groceries. Squad car out front. Cya about 12.

He was bringing food. That was nice.

Oh heck, who was she kidding? This wasn't some garden party. She rolled over, turning away from the phone.

She couldn't think. Her head swam with thoughts of the fact that she needed protection. Her? A librarian. A gigantic waste of time. Add to that the delicious images of what happened the prior night invaded her mind like a dirty movie.

How could a man with the manners and mentality of a brute make her feel so good? A big, tough, rough-around-the-edges bad boy.

She pulled the pillow over her face and screamed into it.

What she wouldn't give to be able to talk to her bestie right now. But aside from that one quick chat, she couldn't call Skye. And it was killing her.

"Skye, I wish you were here."

She threw back the covers and stomped to the bathroom. Why was her body betraying her like this? She needed to date a nice man. Someone who went to church and didn't cuss. Someone she would be proud to introduce to her parents

Oh geez! Now she was just judgmental and rude.

He'd been considerate in other ways. He'd built a new bookshelf for the church. Not only that, but he also didn't have to help Reed. He could've just arrested the guy when he found him. And how many times had he said she deserves to feel good? To have a man cherish her?

She stepped into the shower, praying for some clarity.

He *did* have some redeeming qualities, like complimenting her intellect and taking her out to eat.

She'd have to admit she rather enjoyed cooking for him. She even convinced him to bring over his laundry so she could wash his clothes. Just to be helpful. Living out of a suitcase must have been difficult for him. The masculine smell emanating from his shirts did funny things to her insides.

If Skye *were* here, what would she say?

Lynnie, he's a man, you're a woman. Two consenting adults. Why not enjoy this brief time together. You don't have to analyze everything.

"Ah!" Of course, she did. That was her nature. She couldn't change that any more than a man could change his tattoos.

She snorted.

She toweled off and walked to her closet for fresh

panties and a bra. Then she slipped on her blue jeans. They were snug, but they were so soft. She loved soft things.

She reached for an oversized sweater and stopped.

"Wait a minute," she told the comfortable fabric like it could hear her.

She'd been thinking about this all wrong. He wasn't a bad boy. *No*. He was an ancient fighter, a Norse warrior. He was scruffy, rough and strong, like a warrior. He was a hero. Helping those less fortunate. Saving damsels in distress, and all that.

The epiphany hit her like an avalanche.

"Okay, Skye. Let's try your way."

She sifted through her closet, the hangers squealing in glee from the unused side of the clothes rod

She smiled at the universe, finally ready to take the next step.

CHAPTER 24

JACE HAD BENCHED, pulled, dead-lifted, and sweated out as much frustration as he could that morning at the local YMCA, hoping like hell he could remain a calm, clear-headed adult around Lynée.

After a quick return to his motel for a shower, he went to the grocery store and gathered some food she might enjoy eating. Just about anything, he'd noticed. He loved how she would eat anything and everything, along with a healthy vegetable at every meal. Everything was good to her. He chuckled softly to himself. That was Lynée, in a nutshell, seeing the good in everything. He found it refreshing after years with an agency dealing with crime and maliciousness day after day.

She was a breath of fresh air in a stale and cruel world. Her innocence was surprising and adorable. The way her smile lit up her face made him want to do anything he could to see that a million times over.

But that expectation was unrealistic since he'd be wrapping up and heading back home. To Detroit. Though, he didn't really consider Detroit home. He was rarely there, always on the road following cases.

At checkout, the store had a display of flowers in a fancy tub. A bouquet of gerber daisies, light pink and white ones, caught his eye. Delicate and beautiful, just like her.

Sure, why not?

He had the clerk slide an extra bag over the top to cover the blooms, and he made his way to his bike.

She'll like them. And maybe keep her mind off having a cop car in front of her house hours at a time.

After the short drive, he arrived at her house, rehearsing one last time the rules of engagement for his research assistant.

When she opened the door, he nearly stumbled over his size thirteens.

Lynée stood before him in dark red, body-hugging knit dress, no glasses, long hair in soft ringlets, and makeup that made her lips look more enticing than fresh cherries.

"Wow," was all he could manage. The sound he heard was either his heart slamming against his ribcage or his rules incinerating in a puff of smoke.

Fuck me!

"Thanks. These for me?" she asked with a smile. She reached for the flowers, smelling the pink gerbers. He picked up the subtle hint of rose from her perfume. How fitting a fragrance for her. "Wow. You didn't have to do that."

"Are you...going somewhere?" he asked. No way did she get all dolled up like that just to do more research. Not for him.

"No."

He followed her into the kitchen.

"Should we have a little lunch before we start work?" she asked as she started to unpack the groceries. Her ass in that dress was unbelievable, the most-perfect curve. The urge to kneel at her feet and bite those cheeks consumed him. Work was the last thing on his mind. The dick in his pants vetoed that the moment she opened the door.

Get a grip, Ivy.

He cleared his throat. "Sounds good. There's lunch meat or hamburger meat in there."

"Great."

She pulled down a vase and arranged the flowers, filling it with water. Then she smelled the blooms again. "These are so sweet." She turned toward him, her smile so tender.

"The least I could do for inconveniencing you."

"You are not an inconvenience." She rested her hands on his chest and lifted on her tiptoes.

He leaned down to help close the gap for her.

"Thank you," she whispered against his cheek, kissing above his beard.

He couldn't help himself. He wrapped an arm around her, drawing her closer.

Her kiss lingered, her breath floating over his ear.

He returned the kiss to her cheek, savoring her curvy body pressed against his. "You're welcome." He should let go, get back to work. But he held her longer, breathing in her rosy scent. She didn't pull away either; just let him envelop her in his arms. She was so soft, so responsive to his touch. A long moment passed before he released her.

He turned away. Because he didn't trust his hands to behave. "I'm going to check a few things on the computer real quick."

He had to put distance between them. He didn't know why she'd dressed the way she did, but damn if it didn't make him as hard as a rock. Showing off her curves made him want to strip that dress off her body and explore every blessed curve God gave her.

While she prepped lunch, he perused the online game,

Dark Inferno, that Monroe had connected with the cartel...hoping something would jump out at him to connect the dots. Lynée hadn't been kidding; there were so many contacts, so many drops made in only a few months. The amount of money involved was staggering.

She called him to the table for lunch. Thank the heavens above because his stomach growled loudly, easily heard from the kitchen.

She giggled. "I hope I made enough."

The workout this morning really built up my appetite.

He looked at his plate. Two sandwiches, a bowl of potato soup, apple slices, a pickle spear, and a tall glass of milk. This woman knew how to tame the beast.

He sent her a wink. "This should hold me."

They ate in amiable silence. She sat across from him, her back to the window with the sunlight streaming in around her hair. He finally asked the question burning on his mind. "Bell, why are you all dressed up? Don't get me wrong, you look amazing. It's just unexpected."

She swirled the spoon around her soup and smoothed her lips together. She spoke so softly, he barely heard her say, "I thought you would like it."

"You thought—" He was speechless. His words from the prior day replayed in his mind. To pleasure her with his mouth. He leaned on his elbow closer to her and pulled her soft hand to his lips. He kissed her palm and watched her face.

Her eyelids fluttered closed. He kissed the inside of her wrist, the rose scent intensifying. "Bell, do you want what I offered yesterday?"

She swallowed again and could barely meet his eyes. "Yes," she whispered.

"I can't hear you."

She met his gaze straight on. "Yes, I want that. I want all of it." She set down her spoon. "Please."

Fuck me!

He stared at her, weighing his options, which weren't many. He kissed her palm again and lowered himself to his knees. He pulled her chair out to face him.

She gasped but didn't stop him. He stroked his hands up and down her thighs, moving her legs to make room for him to shuffle between them.

His hands reached up to cup her cheeks, running a thumb over her bottom lip. He leaned forward and placed a kiss on her full lips. He slid her hips closer to him on the chair. Bringing the junction of her thighs flush up against him.

"Oh," she called out in surprise.

"Bell, I would love nothing more than to give you what you want." He tilted his head and kissed her harder, claiming her mouth with his tongue and savoring the taste of her.

Her arms draped around his neck.

He wrapped his arms around her waist and stood.

Her voice was breathless. "You carry me like I weigh nothing more than those flowers."

"You're prettier than the flowers."

He carried her to her bedroom and set her down by the bed, caressing her arms down to her wrists. Her skin was like silk and the color of fresh cream. He reached down, gathering her dress slowly to pull it off.

She stood before him in a baby pink satin bra and panties. Like a second skin, with thin straps that barely looked like they were there. Her cleavage called to him, beckoning him forward to massage them.

I'm a goner! "Bell, you are so beautiful." He lowered

his lips to her neck, kissing her neck down to her clavicle. "You are men's fantasy."

Her breath grew louder. Her hands came around his shoulders, lightly holding him as he worshipped her body.

He teased her gorgeous nipples peaked beneath her bra. He had to taste them. He snaked an arm behind her and unclipped her bra, watching her face for any sign of hesitation.

She simply watched him, her eyes growing a deeper emerald.

The garment fell to the ground, along with his jaw. Those breasts were the most perfect set he'd ever laid eyes on. The rosy nipples were hardened into tiny nubs. He captured them with his large hands, taking one pointed nipple into his mouth.

Her hands dug into his shoulders, and she pressed her chest forward.

"I'm going to enjoy watching you take all the pleasure I can give, Bell. Lay on the bed."

She pulled the comforter back and crawled to the center.

He whipped off his T-shirt and jeans and quickly fished out a condom from his back pocket. His dick felt some relief, but it wasn't nearly enough.

This gorgeous woman, his Tinkerbell, lay before him wearing nothing but panties, asking him to make her feel good. To make her climax like she never had before.

Hands straddling her, he hovered over her, kissing her perfect full lips.

She opened and let him feast. Her mouth was made to tempt and tease a man, and he only hoped he might see how much more. But not now. This time was all about her.

His kisses traveled to her breasts, savoring their

sumptuous weight and taste. Soft and plump, flushed and fleshy, all for him.

She writhed under his sucking and nibbling, and the gentle smell of her started to fill the air.

He traveled further south, admiring her belly button and sweet skin, then licking the edge of her lacy panties.

With his gaze on her face, he gripped the sides of the garment and dragged them down.

She lifted her hips, her mouth gaping. Her chest rose and fell faster, and her cheeks were as pink as cherry blossoms.

He glided a finger over her mons, the strawberry blonde curls trimmed short.

She moaned when his finger slid down between her lips. Already dripping for him.

He kissed her belly, her thighs, and finally, her perfect pussy. So sweet, almost buttery that melted in his mouth. He growled at his first taste of her. God, she was like honey, and he was fucking hungry.

"Jace," she moaned. Her hands gripped his head.

His tongue licked, laved, and roamed, taking in all of her. Relishing every inch. He returned to her hard clit, pressing and massaging with a flat tongue.

With barely any warning, she cried out her orgasm. Her clit pulsed under his tongue, and a surge of sweet nectar rewarded his efforts.

He wasn't nearly done. He laid an arm over her belly while his mouth continued its relentless assault. Slowly, he inserted a finger, turning and twisting.

She bucked more against the mattress, mewling as he focused on bringing her to another climax. He added a second finger, stroking her core, feeling her muscles contract around him. He loved how incredibly responsive she was to his touch.

"Jace," she called out, riding the waves of another explosion.

His dick screamed for a release, her mewls and moans like a carnal aphrodisiac. He couldn't wait any longer. He rose, licked his lips, and lowered his boxer briefs.

Lynée's eyes rounded. "Oh, Jace. I don't think my body can take that."

He sheathed himself and lowered over her, his hands cupping her face. "I'll go slow, baby, I promise."

She nodded, and he kissed her precious mouth, anxious to fill her completely.

"Now, roll over, my Bell."

She did, and his hands instantly went to her glorious, round ass. He kissed and licked each globe like he might never get the chance again. Then he pushed one bent leg to the side, opening her to him. He crawled up behind her, brushing his left leg against hers.

He kissed below her ear. "Bell, I'm going—"

"Say my name," she cooed.

"Lynée. Sweet Lynée..." He licked the shell of her ear. He aligned his cock at her entrance. "We'll start slow, then when your body is used to me, we'll go faster. When you say the word, I'm going to fuck you harder than any other man has."

Her body shivered in his hands, and she nodded.

He slowly pushed inside. Her heat was so intense, wrapping around his dick like a fist. He could feel every inch of her warm wet channel. The pulsing throughout his body escalated. "Fuck, you are so tight."

She moaned long and low as he pushed another few inches inside her recesses.

"How is that, baby?" His voice was strained.

"Yes...oh, yes, more."

He laced his fingers with hers, pressing into the mattress as he pumped into her delicious pussy, in and out, slowly picking up rhythm. Each time he plunged in, he went farther. Stretching her, molding her to his cock. "Lynée," his breath labored, "you feel incredible. I could fuck you all day."

Her pussy muscles clenched around him until he was finally seated deep inside her. He paused a moment for fear of blowing his wad any second.

After he composed himself, he pushed in again. His tough skin gliding over creamy, soft skin was enough to make him shudder, even through a condom.

Her full, round ass lifted slightly to his thrusts.

He picked up speed, feeling confident she'd adjusted to his size. He moved his hands to her hips, gripping on tight to control the tempo.

"Harder, Jace. Please."

Fuck me! When they started, he didn't know if she'd ever reach this point, where she'd ask for it harder, like a greedy sex kitten. But he'd hoped for it. Now she'd said the word—*harder*—and it was like opening a quarter horse's starting gate.

He pumped, his balls slapping against her clit as he pistoned into her core. He prayed she was close again, he didn't have much time.

The beginning contractions of her orgasm gripped his cock and pulled him in. He arched back and thrust again.

She screamed out just as he released his climax, and he came seemingly without end. His nuts drew up so hard, an insane torrent of ecstasy rushed through his body. He continued pumping into her until the wave was over, and his body couldn't hold up his own weight.

He collapsed over her, both of them panting.

"Oh my gosh, Jace."

He lifted slightly. "Are you okay?"

"More than okay. That was incredible."

It was. But why? He'd been with a lot of women. Tall, stacked, voluptuous women, and in the same position. Somehow, he couldn't remember any of them right now. Nor did he want to. Lynée had erased them from his memory. She was the cream of the crop.

CHAPTER 25

LYNÉE LAY ON her side, opening her eyes to the sunshine of a new day. Focus took longer since she'd slept in her contacts.

Jace spooning her with warmth from behind. His breathing even and deep.

She gently moved to her back, appreciating the soreness from deep inside. How long had it been since her body felt so used, so worshiped? Maybe never.

Jace had shifted to his back, his face so serene, still asleep. The man took up most of her queen-sized bed. She scanned his body, his powerful chest, his ridged abs, and those long, talented fingers. His tattoos shifted as his chest rose and fell so peacefully.

Do they have any meaning?

The sheet covered the lower half of his body, and she wondered how he could stay warm in the winter uncovered like that.

The events of the prior night replayed in her head. The way Jace had kissed her, touched her, licked her—how could sex be so incredible? She'd lost count of how many orgasms he'd given her.

Her heart rate picked up, imagining what he looked like under the sheet.

She bit on her lip. She couldn't. She *shouldn't.*

Darn it!

Gripping the covers at her neck with one hand, she gently lifted the sheet to reveal a hip, but not enough to wake him.

She raised them a bit more, revealing dark curls and the top of his beautiful cock.

Oh my.

Was it her imagination, or was it growing?

He groaned. She froze.

"Bell, unless you're ready for round five, you might want to stop now." His deep voice rasped with sleep.

Lynée quickly brought her hands together at her chest. She flushed at the idea of another round with him but also knew they couldn't. She was too sore.

"Uh, good morning."

He opened his eyes. "Good morning to you, Miss Insatiable."

"I'm not. Maybe just a little curious." Her voice dipped.

He grinned. "Bell, I heard you scream with every orgasm. I felt your pussy contract every time I said 'fuck.' You begged for more."

She gasped. "No."

"Yes." He chuckled. "And it was the most glorious thing I've ever heard. The best I've ever felt."

Oh no. Was he right? Did she like dirty talk? Her body clearly did. As much as she didn't want to admit it.

Moisture gathered at the apex of her thighs.

Change the subject.

"Why do you always call me Bell?"

He shifted to his side and ran a fingertip over her lips. "Your lips. Remind me of Tinkerbell. Their perfect, adorable shape."

She blinked. She'd never really thought about it.

"Does it bother you?"

"No." If she was completely honest with herself…"I like you saying my name. The nickname, too."

He tucked a strand of hair behind her ear, his stare full of tenderness. "You're so unassuming, so honest and beautiful." He paused and gave her a quick peck on the mouth, then threw back the covers. "I better put some clothes on, or we'll never get out of this bed." He headed for the bathroom.

She watched his tight, round ass walk away and hide behind the closed door.

She exhaled, warmth flooding her cheeks. He was right. Just talking to him, being close, remembering everything she'd experienced the last night, made her want more.

But holy Moses, she missed her best friend something awful. If she could help Jace, she could get Skye back. Of course, that would mean Jace would leave, but she simply couldn't think about that now.

She slipped out of bed and slid on her robe. Time for coffee, breakfast, and more research. *I need my friend back and my life back to normal.*

Jace returned to the computer after a delicious evening delight.

Damn. A lot can change in a week.

He was in her bed the prior night. Her gorgeous body, all that smooth skin, naked and his for the taking. And fuck, did he take. He couldn't get enough of her. He was like a horny teenager.

Where the fuck did this come from?

Sitting there, reading a file of all the DEA login ID's

164

who'd entered the system last October, and he couldn't focus for shit. He wanted Lynée again.

But he'd had his taste. He gave her an unforgettable night like he'd promised. Now he needed to leave her alone. She didn't belong to him. This incredible woman needed someone just as giving, with morals up the kazoo. She needed a gentle man, not a brute. All of her dreams deserved to come true, including children and a place to call home.

He shifted on the sofa, punching the back cushions, trying to get comfortable.

Ah fuck!

He picked up the cell phone resting on the table. He knew who to call that may have answers.

"Who are you calling?" Lynée called from the kitchen.

"Reed."

Her eyes widened. "Can I talk to Skye?"

Shit! How could he say no to that face?

Monroe answered on the second ring.

"Ivy, what's wrong?"

"Nothing. Reed, do you happen to recall what level of administrators can edit logged files on the system? Do you know who grants those access levels?"

After a short conversation about it—with little insight from Monroe—he gave in to his scattered brain and looked at Lynée. Practically bouncing on her toes.

Jace handed her the phone. *Finally.*

"Skye, oh my gosh. I miss you."

"Lynnie, I miss you too. How are you?" Her voice sounded so happy.

"Wait, you first."

"We're fine. I've learned I'm very good at Monopoly."

"*Cheater*," she heard Reed in the background.

Skye laughed.

"You sound good."

"We are. Some days we're bored, but I'm so glad to be here with Reed. Aside from having to hide out, I am so insanely happy, I can't tell you. How are things with Jace? Is he making you crazy?"

Lynée discreetly took her coat off the hook, slipped it on, and ducked out the back door. "Well, um, good. Really good."

"Oh, I'm happy to hear that. I'm surprised. The way you two were at each other's throats when you dropped us off, I expected you'd have tied his balls in knots by now."

Lynée chuckled, but secretly the thought of touching Jace's balls...Oh, dear. "The thing is, he's been, well, really nice."

Her bestie paused. "Nice? That's good."

She could no doubt sense Lynée had more to tell. But why was it so difficult? Why couldn't she just blurt it out? *Jace and I had sex.*

"Care to expound on that?" Skye nudged.

Through the window, Jace was washing his hands at the kitchen sink. Coast was clear for girl talk. "Gosh, Skye, it's like nothing I've ever experienced. He told me I deserved a man who worships me. Then he offered to help me feel good, to just say the word."

She gasped. "No?"

"Yes. Skye, he bent me over the counter and his fingers..." Her body clenched in pleasure at the memory. "Wow."

"Holy crap, Lynnie. Good for you."

"And last night," she wrapped her arm across her chest, as if trying to hold in the bliss, "we had sex."

"Finally! Good for you, sister. How was it?"

166

Her cheeks felt so hot under her palms. "Awesome. Out of this world. I'm sore today." One more peek inside, and her personal bodyguard was still right there...watching. "It's like he knows just what I like. How to touch me and everything. I never knew it could be like this."

"Lynnie, I'm so happy for you. This was sooo overdue. Please enjoy it. Do more of it, okay?"

More? "You think so?"

"Yes, absolutely. Enjoy this while you can. Look, I know you want to get me—get us—out of here. For that, I'm grateful. But I know you. You'll bury yourself in research and not come up for air. Take breaks. Naked breaks."

Lynée laughed, and Skye joined in. Her friend was probably right.

"I better go. Reed is giving me the eye. Hopefully, you can call me again soon. I love you."

"I love you too." She ended the call.

Skye told her not to stop. Maybe one night wasn't enough. Maybe a little more of Jace would be good for her. To show her what she wanted in future relationships.

She furrowed her brows. She didn't want to think about dating anyone just now. Not anyone *else,* anyway.

CHAPTER 26

JACE WATCHED LYNÉE serve a shrimp and pasta dish. This woman was a damn good cook. Whichever man she ends up with someday should be wildly ecstatic.

"Care for garlic bread?"

"Does a bear sh—" he stopped himself, "poop in the woods?"

She rolled her eyes and set the bread on the side of his plate.

All he could do was chuckle. God, this woman made him laugh. Seriously, he laughed almost every day now. When was the last time he'd experienced that? Before his dad died?

Didn't matter. This investigation was turning up some incredibly fruitful information. If Carlos even thinks of stepping foot on US soil, DEA could have him locked up for at least a dozen life-sentences. And Jace owed so much of it to Lynée. She'd turned up evidence linking Cabello himself to multiple offshore bank accounts involved in the drug trade, as well as connecting many of his confederates to major drug drops. She even uncovered several bribe payouts to other agencies. A huge shitstorm was about to rain down on a lot of people. The woman was brilliant and funny and serendipitously was a lot less pissed at him.

He chuckled to himself. Only two weeks ago, her buttons were so damn sensitive, and he loved to push them. Look how far they'd both come.

"This is good."

She smiled his way. "I'm glad you like it."

When dinner ended, she stood to gather the dishes. "Why don't you wait here. I have dessert for you."

"I always have room for dessert." He smiled.

After a few short minutes, Lynée returned. Her shirt missing.

"Oh, hell."

Standing beside the table, she wore only snug faded jeans and a black and purple bra. She'd ditched the oversized sweater.

He loved what she was advertising now.

She stalked toward him, slowly dipping to her knees in front of him, grabbing the chair like he'd done twice before to her. The chair didn't budge when she tugged.

He wanted to laugh how adorable she was.

"Help me out?" she asked playfully.

He scooted the chair to the side to face her.

Her hands rested on his knees as she slid them apart to shimmy between. "I'm giving a different kind of dessert tonight. Would you like to try it? This recipe is new to me." She shrugged.

Damn! This wonderful woman was going to pleasure him tonight with her innocent, perfect mouth. His dick grew several inches, threatening to pop a stitch of his jeans.

"I have zero doubt that I will love whatever you give, Bell."

She smiled wide. Her hands roamed up his jean-clad thighs. Licking her lips with concentration, she went to his button and zipper, and with a little fumbling, unfastened everything.

He shifted to help her reveal his impatient cock.

She gripped the waistband of his briefs and reached in to take hold.

Fuck me!

Her delicate hands were like heaven wrapped around his hungry dick. He swallowed hard.

Those beautiful pink lips leaned down and wrapped around his tip.

He groaned and let his head drop back.

She poked his slit with her tongue then laved at the underside, all the way down and all the way up. Sending jolts of energy through his body. Her tongue slipped up and over and around, never breaking away. Until her lips joined in. Wrapping tightly around the head, sliding up and down in concert with her fist.

The heat...the pressure...

"Fuck," he breathed out. He opened his eyes long enough to take in the sight. His Tinkerbell on her knees, worshiping him with her puffy pink lips and looking up at him with beautiful green doe-eyes. This image would be branded on his mind forever.

The familiar tug on his nuts signaled the building inferno. He didn't have much time left.

He stroked her cheek in silent praise, savoring the big force from that little mouth. "Bell," he panted, "I'm about to blow. You may want to back away."

But the vixen wouldn't have it. She stroked and sucked harder.

Oh hell! He slammed his eyes shut and rode the monsoon wave that crashed through him. He growled through his release, as she squeezed the last drop from him.

With hazy eyes, he looked down at his Bell, watching

her swallow and lick him one last time.

He was vaguely aware of her putting him back together, still drunk on the post-orgasmic euphoria.

"Dear God, Bell. Where did you learn that?" Although the second the question was out of his mouth, maybe he didn't want to know.

"I told you. I read. A lot." Her self-satisfied grin was well-earned.

He leaned forward, cupping her jaw and drawing her in. He claimed those precious, talented lips with the most insane feeling of gratitude he'd ever had.

He pulled back, meeting her gaze. "I have plans for us tomorrow. A little break. So when I come over in the morning, I want you wearing just your robe."

Her cheeks bloomed with color. "You're not spending the night?"

"Not tonight. I have something to do." He rose and took her hand and then helped her to her feet. "But remember. The morning."

She nodded and bit on her bottom lip.

He kissed her long and hard one last time. Then as he did every night, "Lock up behind me," and he pulled her front door closed.

Jace walked out of Lynée's house to his bike...on autopilot. His mind was a useless pile of jelly, sated and spent. He strapped on his helmet and could only think of Lynée's fingers working his belt.

What was she doing to him?

This surprising woman had him in foreign territory. It was like a new level of awareness about things, a new level of interest. He simply couldn't define it, but he knew he wanted more. For as long as it would last, he *had* to have more.

He retrieved his phone from his back pocket and waved at Simon in the patrol car. A quick search gave him just what he was looking for. With a press of a button, his Harley came alive.

***

Lynée's palms turned sweaty, gripping her coffee cup.

Holy cannoli, Jace would arrive at any moment, and she couldn't wait. She'd dreamt about him the prior night, evidenced by hot cheeks and a newly familiar ache between her legs. Although she slept hard, she woke up an hour earlier than usual, ready to tackle the world.

She nibbled a fingernail absently. What was it about this man? He made her want more, to see more and try more. Good gravy, she'd gone down on her knees and took him in her mouth. And it was so crazy hot. Seriously, the most exhilarating thing she'd ever done.

She stood in her kitchen, sipping coffee, in her bathrobe, as if it were like any other day.

But it wasn't.

Is this normal?

She had no frame of reference. Things with Todd were good, but nothing like this. They were more safe and content. With Jace, it was like bottle-rockets and sparklers igniting inside and not a soul around to witness the immensity of it. She wanted to scream it out to the world.

This was all so new. Like a strange glow from deep inside.

She needed a distraction. Thanksgiving was around the corner. She could host Thanksgiving dinner, praying Skye and Reed would be back by then. She pulled out her notepad and pen from the drawer and began to write a grocery list.

When the doorbell rang, she nearly jumped. She set down her pen and forced her feet to walk at an even pace toward the door.

Jace wore his usual denim and leather, his eyes deep chocolate as he scanned her from head to toe. Her stomach flipped. Without missing a beat, he scooped her in his arms.

She wrapped her arms and legs around him to hold on.

His lips crashed down on hers as he kicked the door close. He swung her around and pressed her against the door with the mere strength of his body, pinning her, body to body.

She pushed off his leather jacket from his shoulder. She did it to the other as he switched arms holding her. It amazed her how light she seemed in his arms.

Her hands instantly went to his chest, then his abs, tugging on his T-shirt to gain access to his hard body. She roamed freely, pushing his shirt higher.

"Tell me you have nothing on beneath that robe, sweetheart. Because all I could think about was you naked, spread out on your bed, flush from an orgasm," he murmured against her neck.

"See for yourself," she whispered, just as anxious.

He leaned back just enough to pull apart the tie at her waist, then yanked the fabric apart.

"Fuck me. Bell, your body is mine for the next hour." He lifted her higher, bringing his hot mouth to her achy nipple.

"Ah," she panted. *Yes*. This was just what she wanted. She had no idea she could want a man so much. She'd always been rather shy, raised to go after her dreams as quietly as possible. But with Jace, he helped her learn to *want* to be loud. To be reckless, even.

After Jace left, she may have an immense feeling of

guilt, but for now, she wanted to savor everything he could give her. Could teach her.

Jace hauled her off the wall and made his way to the living room sofa. He set her on the cushions and, kneeling at her feet, kissed her again, long and deep.

She broke the kiss, panting, looking into his dark, sparkling eyes. "I want to undress you."

"Be my guest."

She pushed on his T-shirt, raising it over his etched abs to his broad chest.

He took it from there, grabbing the garment and sending it flying.

Her hands roamed his chest, fascinated by the sheer power the man held. So strong, yet so gentle with her. His silver cross sparkled at her. The metal was warm as she twirled the chain between her fingers. She placed several kisses on his pecs while her fingertips continued to explore.

A low growl escaped from deep in his throat.

She rose from the sofa and stepped around him, kissing his bicep, until she finally had a closeup view of his back. The vastness of his tattoos like art on display in a museum. She kissed him several more times. She never knew she could appreciate such...artwork.

Her fingertips traced the intricate design, fascinated by the intricacy. "Do they mean anything?"

"A bit. It's evolved over the years. The shield represents a crusader. My father could see that in me, even though I didn't see it myself. There are a few military symbols. The vines, of course, for Ivy." He shrugged a shoulder.

"How long did it take?"

"Several months." He moaned at her soft hands. "Bell, I've been looking forward to this since yesterday."

She circled around to his front and started to work on his belt and fly. "Then we better not delay another minute."

He helped her push against his jeans and briefs, and he rose to strip them off. Then he grabbed the lapels of her robe and pulled the garment to the floor. She stood naked in front of him.

Normally, this would frighten her half to death. Sex in her living room. Even though all the curtains were drawn, anyone could knock and catch them in the middle of it. But the glow in Jace's eyes, the appreciation, gave her confidence not to be scared. She felt like a powerful, desired woman with Jace. She'd never felt that before.

"Jace."

"I know, Bell, let me take you in." He cupped the back of her neck and nibbled on her lips before diving in for more. A slow, passionate kiss he'd given her several times. She knew he was in no rush to plow through the day.

His kisses traveled down her neck to her breasts, licking and suckling at each nipple as his hands massaged her hips.

The slickness at her sex grew with each caress. She'd never experienced this deep yearning before, only with Jace.

"Sit on the couch, Bell."

She did as he asked.

He knelt before her again, and with his hands on her thighs, stroking gently, he pushed her legs apart.

Cupping her breast, he sucked in a nipple and toyed with the hard peak while his fingers caressed his thighs.

The ache between her legs intensified. Jace languished over her other breast, but his fingers never ventured where she needed him most.

"Bell, I could lose myself in your breasts every night," he murmured against her skin.

She leaned back, resting her palms on the cushion, letting her head drop back and savoring the blessed torture.

His hands and lips never stopped moving, slowly exploring her body in the most delicious way. His kisses then traveled south, over her belly and along the inside of her thighs, finally stopping over her core.

"Mm. Jace."

He laved through her center to her clit, leisurely massaging her little nub, compelling it to grow under his touch. As he inserted a finger, she nearly lost her mind.

He teased her mercilessly for several moments, before grabbing her hips and pulling her forward to the edge, where he had more access.

Holy Moses! She couldn't remember ever feeling so exposed, not that it mattered. The pressure at her sex grew to new heights, and a small trickle escaped.

She watched his face as Jace laid claim to her sex—his tongue exciting her clit, his fingers exploring her depths. He looked like he'd just dived into heaven.

The sensations overwhelmed her, and she squirmed under his attention, trying to keep from climaxing too soon. He knew exactly what her body responded to most, and he exploited it mercilessly.

Those intense coffee eyes looked up at her, his mouth still suckling her center. Those irises practically teased her, daring her to burst on his tongue. And that was it. His eyes were all it took before the flood gates broke free. Her orgasm crashed through her nerve endings and exploded, the current carrying to every corner of her body.

"Jace!" she cried.

He removed his fingers and kissed her skin as her panting slowly calmed.

The familiar sound of a condom wrapper pulled her

eyes open.

In a beat, he turned her body to lay completely flat on the couch. He hovered over her, kneeling just below her. The lust in his eyes matched the flush of his cheeks. So stunning. His hands clasped her knees. As he held her gaze, he slowly pushed inside her and groaned.

She reached for his strong round shoulders, pulling him to her lips. The connection exquisite as he moved inside her, gently rocking.

"Jace," she breathed over his lips.

"Don't think, Bell. Just feel."

That was all she could do. This was nothing like she'd ever felt before. She swore Jace actually touched her soul as well. Caressed and cherished her soul.

As he dove in deeper, sweat gathered on his brow. "Are you okay?" His voice shook.

She wasn't able to find her voice at all. All she could do was nod because any second she'd start to cry. This rapturous feeling was almost too much. The coil tightened so strong inside her, there was no hope for it. She let go of her orgasm, letting it wash over her like some glorious gift from heaven.

Jace dropped his head in the crux of her neck, his beard caressing her skin. He growled from his own climax.

When he pulled out, he shifted her to cradle her from behind and wrap her into his warm naked body. They lay together in silence on the sofa, regaining their balance on the world, and holding back reality for a little longer. Any words at this point would dull the moment between them.

In her mind, she knew. He touched her deep inside and opened up a love that had been trapped inside for years.

But she didn't dare speak that aloud. Jace would go back to his career and leave Cascade Creek, and she would have to find a way to move on. For now, all she could do was stroke his arms swaddled around her breasts.

Jace broke the silence, his breath hot against her ears. "I don't want you to go anywhere without me. I don't want you alone at any point."

She stopped. "What? Why not?"

His arms tightened around her. "It's not safe, Lynée. Promise me. Nowhere without me."

Processing his words took her a few extra seconds. He'd gone back to protector-mode; she forced herself not to feel like a supervised child. "Okay."

He raised up on his arm and pecked the top of her head. "Thank you. Now, put on some warm clothes." He lifted his insanely toned and muscular body off her sofa to dispose of the condom and retrieve his jeans. "Do you have a leather jacket?"

What? "Um, yeah."

"Great. Wear that too."

"Where are we going?"

"You'll see." He grinned. Combined with his tousled hair and plump lips, the combination nearly took her breath away. Again.

She grabbed her robe from the floor and retreated upstairs to dress. Her puffy jacket was warmer for the winter, but she relented and pulled her leather coat from her closet, along with a fresh pair of jeans and a cashmere sweater. A few minutes later, she walked into the living room to find Jace standing by the door.

"Beautiful. All set?"

"Now, will you tell me where we're going?" She hooked her bag over her shoulder.

"You won't need that."

"But I need my license."

He stepped closer and stroked the back of his hand down her cheek. "Trust me. Leave it here."

Okay, now he had her worried.

After locking the door behind her, she looked to the curb. There sat Jace's motorcycle, as it had before. But now a pink and white helmet rested on the seat. She didn't need a Ph.D to figure out the helmet was for her. Her steps slowed. "Oh Jace. I really have no interest in riding a motorcycle."

He moved in and wrapped his arm around her waist, drawing her into his hips. "Babe, we'll just go for a little drive, maybe into the mountains a bit. We'll take it slow. I would love to take you for a spin on my bike. Something I love and want to share with you."

She fell speechless. She had the distinct feeling this was a big deal for him. Sweat accumulated inside her gloves.

"You'll be holding onto me." He grinned, his stare so playful.

Oh geez. "Okay. Maybe just around the block." She rubbed her lips together as he slipped on the helmet and tightened the strap.

Breathe.

Lynée was the farthest thing from a daredevil. She preferred to play it safe. One summer, during her short marriage, Todd wanted to take her to the amusement park and ride the tallest rollercoaster. He said it would be fun. Not for her. Rollercoasters were scary. They'd gone on a kayaking trip instead. How Jace was able to so easily talk her into riding with him, she might never understand.

"You look like a badass in this helmet." He winked.

"Oh, the pink does it for you, huh?"

"Combined with the black leather jacket, hell yeah." He

mounted the bike. "Okay. Get on from the left side. Put your foot here." He pointed to the peg by the rear tire.

Am I really about to do this?

She took a deep breath, placed her left foot on the peg, and swung her right leg over the seat.

"Very good. Now, wrap your arms around my waist."

She slipped her arms around his middle, and breathed in the manly leather scent, a unique combination with his cologne.

He raised her hand to his lips and planted a quick kiss on her knuckles.

The bike started, the engine roaring to life between her legs. The whole thing vibrated through her entire body.

Jace maneuvered them to the street. She gripped his jacket with all her might as he took off down the road. To his credit, he took it slow, just as he'd promised.

They drove around the block a few times, and eventually, her arms relaxed. He asked if she was ready to try another route, and she agreed. They climbed into the mountains, weaving along up the side, breathing in the freshest air in the country. When the tall evergreens thinned out, more of the snow-capped mountain range came into view. The brilliant, crisp majesty of it all was positively breathtaking.

"How ya' doing?" he called back to her.

"Beautiful," Lynée answered. The longer they drove, the more at ease on the motorcycle she became. Her grip wasn't as tight around his waist, and her face wasn't glued to the back of his shoulder. She probably didn't need to worry. She was with Jace. He'd never let anything happen to her. *That* she knew with all her being.

After driving for an hour, they returned to Cascade Creek for lunch.

Killing the engine and helping her with her helmet, Jace asked, "How was that?"

She beamed, the residual vibrations fading from her legs. "That was incredible. I can see why motorcycle clubs are so popular up here. So free and exhilarating."

He grinned. "I'm glad you liked it. C'mon, let's go eat."

Before she let him move an inch, she threw her arms around him.

He caught her easily, squeezing her back. "Whoa."

"Jace, thank you. That was thrilling."

"Anytime, Bell," he said close to her ear.

CHAPTER 27

LYNÉE'S BODY ACHED in the most beautiful ways, with each step down the stairs. Though the wood floors were cold under her slippers, she was all warm and fuzzy inside. Not just because she was wrapped in her robe. Sublime lovemaking made her feel all alive inside. Sore, but alive.

She started a pot of coffee and planned to spiff up a mountainous breakfast for the mountain of divine muscle still sleeping in her bed. After cracking a few eggs into a bowl and using the last of the milk, the garbage can was full. They'd been otherwise occupied with all the research and sex the previous several days, she'd even missed her trash day.

With a quick change to a fresh liner, she unlocked the back door and dragged the full bag to the garbage can on her patio. The air was frigid, and the morning light was pale, fighting to warm up the world.

Holy cow, Jace had accomplished that for her so perfectly. Warming up her world.

She turned to walk back up the stairs and tripped.

Her body fell forward. Something strong wrapped around her face.

She yelped, but the sound stopped against the gloved hand over her mouth. A jab in her side made her crumple, but her whole body squeezed against a form at her back, keeping her from hitting the ground.

Someone dragged her backward. The paving stone caught her slipper and ripped it off.

"Where are they?" a vicious voice muttered into her ear. The thick accent low and cold, the sound freezing her spine.

She clawed at the oppressive hand over her mouth, pulling her back so hard, she was sure her skin was bruised. Shaking her head didn't loosen his hold, and biting did nothing against the leather gloves. Pleading eyes glued to the back door, willing Jace to follow her outside. To see the intruder and save her. But it was pointless. He was still soundly asleep in her bed.

"Tell me where they are," the voice continued. "And I'll make this quick." The painful jab at her side twisted, and she realized it was the barrel of a gun.

They?

He dragged her farther back toward the gate that led to her garage. Beyond that was the back drive that connected everyone's driveways on the street. She would easily disappear, and no one would ever see.

If she could get her mouth free just enough for Jace to hear her scream, that was her only chance.

"Where are they hiding, *puta*?"

It hit her suddenly. He was talking about Skye and Reed. This was the sicko from the cartel trying to murder her best friend. Now he was using Lynée to find them. Just as Jace had predicted.

She blinked back tears, trying to force her brain to calm down so she could think her way out of this.

The back door opened.

Her heart froze.

Jace's irritated face stepped out. He was shirtless and barefoot but had managed to throw on a pair of jeans. "I thought I told you not to go outside alone, Bell. What are you—"

His gaze caught hers.

In the instant, it took her to scream against the hand, her lover's face paled, and he reached into his back waistband.

Her assailant aimed his weapon at Jace and fired. The bullet went wide and hit the flower pot next to his ankle.

Jace ducked to the side and jumped the steps to hide behind the fence for cover.

The man tightened his grip around her shoulders. The drag backward grew more urgent to find his own cover. She was his human shield. "Come on out, lover boy," he called.

God help her, this was it. This was how everything was going to end. Tears streamed freely from her cheeks. She'd urged Skye into fighting for what she loved and helping Reed. Only to have all of them end up dead from this psychopath.

Get it together, woman. She looked around in her limited scope, forcing herself to calm down and find a way out. If she had to die—if *this* were her last moment on Earth—she would make sure Skye was safe. She would use the very advice she'd given her best friend only a few weeks before. To fight back. To fight for what she loved.

But how?

A car door slammed shut down the street. Seconds later, a different voice called from over the bushes. "Agent Ivy? Miss Clark?"

Sheriff Wyatt.

She screamed again, but nothing went past the man's hand.

From behind the fence, Jace hollered in a commanding voice, "Four-seventeen! The bastard has Lynée!"

Jace called himself every single derogatory name he could think of. He'd let down his guard for one blissful moment, and now the woman he loved had a gun to her head.

Control. Regain control.

He gripped his pistol and forced his mind to focus on procedure. Four-seventeen was the police code for assailant with a gun, but he couldn't remember the one for hostage. At least one blessed thing was going right—he had backup every night at Lynée's house.

From the brief glimpse he'd gotten of Lynée's captor, he was the same man from the bathroom photo. Dark, leathery skin, and even darker, evil eyes. And the same size as Jace, if not an inch or two taller. One big fucker. Holding Lynée like a ragdoll.

Jace's hunch about the cartel coming after her as a way to find Monroe was right. The one damn time he wanted to be wrong...

Tears streamed down her cheeks, her eyes so wide and panicked. Her terrified face twisted his heart like wringing out a rag with steel spikes. No other moment in his life was more horrifying than seeing her in the clutches of this madman.

"Ivy, what's your twenty?" the sheriff called from off to the side.

If he answered that, it would give away his location to the gunmen, too. So he answered the question the sheriff should've asked. "He's by the garage, holding Lynée in front of him."

The unmistakable sound of a crackling radio came off

to his side as the sheriff called in for backup. "Shots fired, hostage situation." He gave the address.

Jace peeked around the other side of the fence for a better vantage point. He moved between bushes, trying to get closer and find a clear shot. All he'd need was one.

Another shot rang out, the bullet zipping by his head. *Damn,* this guy was a good shot.

He ducked behind the neighbor's car, keeping his feet behind the tire. Daring a glance over the trunk, he swallowed hard.

The guy had hauled Lynée behind the garage, his expression gleeful. He muttered something in her ear, though he was too far to hear the words. Whatever he'd said had pissed her off from the fire raging in her eyes. She bucked and wailed, flailing her arms to loosen his hold. The back of her head clocked his chin, and he swore. Dropping his hand from her mouth.

Her scream pierced the air in a sickening sound that amped up his heart rate even more.

A gunshot followed, echoing down the street.

Jace flinched.

"Let her go!" Wyatt called. His bullet missed the bastard and lodged into the garage siding.

Dammit! The sheriff had nearly gotten Lynée. She was struggling and flailing so much; it was too risky to take that shot.

The cartel demon aimed his weapon straight for Wyatt and fired. The sheriff dove back toward his cover spot, but not quick enough. He yelped and grunted behind the fence. Followed by silence.

"Wyatt, call out."

It was a long few seconds before the sheriff finally answered with a strained voice. "I'm hit."

"Fuck," Jace muttered and glanced back at the garage. The prick had dragged Lynée farther down the driveway, making his way toward a car several houses down. She was kicking and thrashing. But that brute was too strong. And massive. His arm only tightened around her mouth to keep her from screaming more. The photo hadn't displayed just how big this monster was.

He aimed at Jace and fired again. The bullet lodged into the other side of the car.

If he made it to his vehicle, getting Lynée back alive would be infinitely harder. He needed her alive, but only long enough for her to get the information he wanted. In whatever painful and gruesome way he could.

The thought enraged Jace to the point of blinding hatred. He had to save her from that torture.

Dammit, just one good shot. That's all I need. Come on, baby.

All of her struggling made the demon's sleeve pull away from his glove. One more thrash, and he slipped. Lynée's mouth clamped down on his wrist, her teeth sinking in.

He howled and yanked his hand back.

Dropping her to the ground.

Jace stood and inhaled. Then fired.

His shot missed.

The guy raised his gun right at him. His gaze glared savage and evil.

Jace fired again.

The bullet went straight through the man's eye. A bright puff of red mist exploded behind his head. His body crumpled beside Lynée.

She skittered away, managing to get to her feet and lunging herself at Jace.

The coconut shampoo in her hair never smelled so sweet. Just as he'd never held anyone so tightly. But he didn't dare take his aim off the bastard's body.

He didn't want to let her go. But he had to. "Go check on Wyatt." He moved forward and kicked the gun out of the guy's hand. Behind him came the distant sound of Lynée calling on the sheriff's radio for an ambulance, her voice shaking.

Standing over the son of a bitch and his bloodied head, he thought the image would've made him feel justified. That right had won over evil once again. Gore had never bothered him before, nor had shooting someone. That was his job, to protect others. But this time, knowing the stakes were the highest he'd ever faced...protecting Lynée...losing Lynée...

He forced himself to step away, the adrenaline pulsing through his veins at a strange pace. Sweat dripped down his face, and the muscles in his jaw worked, grinding his teeth together.

Lynée hunched over Wyatt, with blood splattered on her robe and on her cheek. A red, savage curtain drop over Jace's vision.

The fury in his gut raged to a boil. He turned and made the three steps to Lynée's metal lawn chairs. He easily lifted one over his shoulder and threw it down the driveway. A roar may have escaped his mouth, he wasn't sure. He couldn't hear anything other than the thrumming between his ears. The next chair went flying, crashing against the fence. He grabbed the edge of the wrought iron table and flipped it. The crash wasn't as satisfactory as he'd hoped. He needed to break something.

"Jace! Jace!"

He couldn't quite hear the voice clearly when the third chair bounced off the tree and crashed onto the upturned table.

"Jace Ivy!"

He turned in the direction of his name.

Lynée stood by Wyatt, both of them staring at him. The sheriff's face was pale.

"I need your help here," she said in a calmer tone.

He forced a deep breath, willing his feet to move. His chest heaved from exertion. A glance at the destroyed lawn furniture told him just how badly he'd lost his shit.

Pull it together, Ivy.

"Jace, I need your help with Wyatt," Lynée pleaded.

Right. Wyatt was hit.

He jogged over and bent down to see blood, soaking the man's thigh. He quickly felt for the bullethole and checked for an exit point on the other side of his leg. With two hands, he clamped down on the wound. A groan tore from Wyatt's mouth. "Hang in there. Pressure is your friend right now."

His gaze landed on Lynée, who stared at him, fear written all over her face.

Police sirens sounded in the distance, closing in quickly. Hopefully, the ambulance wasn't too far behind.

Lynée was likely in shock, and Jace's outburst made it worse. *Fuck!*

CHAPTER 28

SHERIFF WYATT HAD suffered a life-threatening shot in the leg, straight through the femoral artery. But he'd survived, the surgery was a success, and he should make a relatively-full recovery. Though his career was probably over, Lynée had overheard the surgeon say.

Countless police and DEA officials had swarmed her house most of the day after she'd returned from the hospital, and she'd had to recount the events several times. Each time more unbearable than the next. Jace had been interviewed by even more people, though he'd stayed as close as possible to her. Constantly hugging her whenever he could, rubbing her back and kissing her forehead.

She got the feeling from the sideways glances of the other DEA agents that maybe he wasn't supposed to be doing that. But he clearly didn't care.

Hours later surveying all the boxes and computer equipment in her house, her muscles still refused to release their tension. And she still couldn't get her hands to stop shaking.

Emilio Cortez.

That had been the cartel assassin's name. Hired for one purpose: find Reed and take him out. He'd killed several people to achieve his goal already, and she had nearly been the latest one.

The only reason she was still alive was because of Jace. The only reason Skye and Reed were still alive as well.

Jace.

Thankfully, he'd already called the other pair and verified they were safe. Her best friend was terrified for Lynée and wanted to return immediately. In her heart, Lynée wanted her back as well. But Jace wouldn't hear of it.

They still hadn't discovered the identity of the mole.

The timeline on the corkboard stared at her, mocking her...they still hadn't finished.

Will this ever end? Will Skye ever be able to come home?

Will Jace leave when that happens?

The sun was setting, and everyone had finally left, Jace locking the door behind them.

Images of him throwing her patio furniture still replayed in her head along with every other horrific scene from the morning. She was spent.

"I need a shower," she announced. Maybe that would help ease the tension in her body. And get her away from a case that she now begrudged. She pulled on the sofa armrest to get herself standing.

"Wait a second." Jace sat beside her and took her hand. "We need to talk about this."

"I know, I shouldn't have gone outside without you, and I'm sorry that all this—"

"No, Lynée. That's not what I..." He gripped her hands tighter. "This was not your fault. You need to know that. So don't apologize." He sighed, his shoulders slumping as though a huge weight sat on his neck. "*I* need to apologize."

"For what? You're the one who saved both Wyatt and me, and that guy can never hurt anyone else again, because of you."

"I meant... after all that."

She swallowed hard. He referred to the rage episode where he destroyed her furniture. Not a topic she expected him to bring up again. But that was obviously the moment where something shifted between them. "You, uh...kind of broke my patio."

"I'm sorry. I thought I was stronger than that."

"You were pretty strong. I didn't know metal could bend like that without extreme heat."

"No, I meant..." He growled and shook his head. Several seconds passed before he began again, his brow furrowed. "I felt helpless watching that asshole manhandle you. I've never been more scared in my life. Then Wyatt, and all the blood on your clothes... It's like a vile rampage bubbled up inside. It was worse when I was a teen, but I guess it never really went away." He rubbed the backs of her hands with his thumbs. "You know I would never hurt you, right?"

"Yes," she whispered. "I was more worried about you than me."

He gave her a small smile, then pulled her close. His arms wrapped around her, the warmth soothing her frazzled nerves.

"Let's get you in the shower."

As he turned on the hot water, she stripped out of her jeans and sweater. The robe and PJ's she'd worn during the attack still sat in the corner of the bathroom from when she'd changed out of them earlier. Bloodstained most of the fabric. She might just burn all that.

The hot stream cascaded down Lynée's body, the water normally a soothing balm for her soul. But not today. Tears streamed from her eyes, carried away by the water.

The thoughts replayed over and over in her mind—the gun at her head, the vicious words, the sound of gunshots—and it ripped her heart. She buried her face in her hands, trying to stem the flow of tears.

The shower curtain pulled back a little. Jace stepped in behind her, instantly enveloping her in his arms once again.

"Bell." The one word was so soothing, equally tormented, with so much passion and empathy and concern in one syllable.

She turned and gazed into his gruff face. The lines around his eyes had deepened, and somehow a few hairs at his temples in this light almost looked gray.

He stroked her back. She rested her head on his shoulder and squeezed him around the middle. Only then when his cock brushed against her stomach did she realize he was naked. Not that it mattered in the least.

Her muscles slowly started to relax, fiber by fiber. All she wanted to do was stand here like this, safe in his arms for the rest of her life. Not think about this morning, the horrors she'd seen or the sound of that man's voice, or the taste of his skin when she bit into his wrist.

She desperately wanted to forget it all. And just be with Jace.

"What can I do?" he asked after a long moment of silence. "How can I make this better?"

"You're doing it."

"And then what?"

She lifted her head and caressed his chest just over his heart. She also desperately didn't want to think about what happened *after*. How she would go on *after* Jace left.

"Then we go to bed."

He opened his mouth to ask another question, but he stopped.

She could practically see the words forming on his lips. *What about tomorrow?* Somehow, he knew not to ask. Not to voice the possibility.

For the first time in her life, she didn't want to know what happened tomorrow.

Between his thumb and forefinger, he lifted her chin to meet his gaze. "Tell me what you're thinking."

She opened her mouth.

I'm thinking I want you to stay. I'm thinking all this time before you arrived, I haven't really been alive. Now that I know what it feels like to really live, I can't bear to lose you. I'll crumble if you leave.

His gaze was so pleading, the beautiful irises nearly glossy. "Just say the words, Lynée."

I'm thinking I love you.

Her heart cinched in on itself. It took all she had not to cry when the realization hit her full on. The fear of losing him was just as strong as her love.

"I'm tired," she finally replied. "Just...hold me while I sleep."

CHAPTER 29

I'LL HOLD YOU forever.

Last night, those words had threatened to come out of his mouth. Dammit, he'd wanted to say them so badly. He could tell Lynée was about to say something similar in the shower, the thoughts swarming in her mind, but for some reason, she didn't say anything.

The whole night, he lay in her bed, spooning her precious body and breathing in her scent. So grateful she was still there, alive and warm. They hadn't said a word to each other.

Not even a 'good morning' when they woke.

Now, he sat in her living room, perusing more files like he had the last week, the tension between them so thick he could barely breathe.

He had no idea what to say to her. But he couldn't leave her side. He had to be in the same room as her, every second.

Is this just a protective thing? He'd nearly lost her, and now he was going overboard with paranoia.

Or was this more?

His fist crumpled the paper in his hand. He didn't realize he'd been holding it that hard. *Fuck.* He smoothed the paper out against the side of the coffee table.

How the hell could he focus after yesterday?

His boss had chewed him out over the phone for not keeping him updated about the change in his case. For having found Monroe and not bringing him in yet. For having the audacity of allowing the cartel to catch up with him and endanger the life of a civilian and injuring the local sheriff. The longer he'd ranted, the more the self-doubt bubbled up inside of Jace. Those same feelings of inadequacy from his teenage years churned inside. He *knew* better. He knew to follow procedure. This was career-ending crap, and the boulder in his gut reminded him of just that. He might have just worked himself out of the DEA.

And all because he had blinders on.

The woman on the other side of the room glued to the computer screen was infinitely more important. He was just having a harder time accepting this new reality.

Just admit it to yourself, you chicken shit. You love her.

"I found it!" She stood from her chair.

He jolted upright and was at her side in seconds. "Found what?"

She sat down again and pointed at the file she opened. "Joe's unfiled reports. He named it Christmas List. I can't believe I missed it. I skipped over this days ago, but got distracted with something else." She scrolled through the file, reading the lines out loud.

"October 2: First contact referenced an 'inside man' protecting them from law enforcement. New contact shut him up with a gut punch. Did not specify which law enforcement, Federale, US Border & Customs, or DEA. No name given. Didn't give a new drop point/time. Said they'd see me on the game. Report filed."

"That's the Dark Inferno game Monroe talked about." Jace gripped the back of her chair.

Lynée nodded and kept reading.

"October 9: My previous reports on internal systems have disappeared. Intel is missing. Concerned someone inside DEA is tampering with our investigation. Could be the 'inside man' they referenced before. Did not file report in case the system is compromised. Will watch my partner more closely since he's the closest one with access to my files. Do not suspect he knows of my secondary location.

October 12: Suspect referenced 'Slugger.' New lead. May be 'inside man.' Setup test to rule out my partner as mole. Nothing back yet."

Jace froze. The word magnified in his gaze and the rest of the screen blurred.

Slugger.

His throat started to close in on itself. "Read that last one again," he rasped.

She did.

Suddenly, all the pieces fit together in his brain. Sliding into place like they were magnets snapping together in a horrible image, followed by a surge of rage. How the hell had he not known all along...

"Slugger...Son of a fucking bitch!"

He whirled and rummaged through a box for a thumb drive.

"What?" she asked, eyes wide.

He held it out to her. "Put that file on this drive. Please." His whole body shook with fury; he had to remind himself to soften his tone toward her. It wasn't her fault the shit had hit the industrial-sized fan.

She took the drive. "You know who Slugger is?"

He ground his teeth together, hard. To keep from

spouting off more obscenities. "Please. Right now."

She scowled and did as he asked as he searched around for his leather jacket and keys.

A minute later, he barreled out the front door, his boots thunking down the patio steps and the thumb drive safe in his pocket. Lynée followed, slipping on the oversized sweater she'd grabbed from the coat hanger by the door.

"Where are you going?" she asked with a hint of fear in her voice. She stopped at the top of the stairs. The ground was wet from a cold rain overnight, and she was only in slippers.

Just before he reached his motorcycle, he turned and went back. Halting at the bottom step. He gave her a hard look. "Don't say anything. To anyone. Not yet. Keep all that stuff safe."

She swallowed hard and drew her lips together in that adorable Tinkerbell look that drove him wild. She took a few steps down, no doubt soaking her slippers.

"Just tell me what's going on. Let me help."

Dammit, he couldn't help himself. His hand reached out, wrapped around the back of her head, and pulled her close. He locked his lips against hers, tasting the sweet honey from her tea. The kiss was needy, rushed, and a bit harsh.

He pulled away and didn't look back. Just hopped onto his bike, fired it to life, and sped off as fast as the tread would allow.

CHAPTER 30

Three Days Later

LYNÉE CARRIED A tray of fresh blueberry muffins into Sheriff Wyatt's hospital room. Bouquets, balloons, and even a few small teddy bears canvassed the space with barely any free counter room for her gift. She knocked on the open door. "Can I come in?"

The man looked up from a stack of papers on a tray poised over the bed. He smiled wide and took off his reading glasses. "You, Miss Clark, are always welcome."

She stepped in and found the open chair on the other side of the bed. The television displayed the news on a soft volume. The man's hair had almost gone completely gray, something she didn't want to focus on. Before the altercation outside her house, he possessed an equal serving of salt and pepper. Perhaps the physical stress of his injury sped up the aging process, making her feel guiltier than she already was.

She set the tray in front of him. "Fresh out of the oven. Your wife told me you love blueberries."

"You didn't have to do this."

"It's the least I could do. After...everything. I never got a chance to thank you."

He waved his hand as if dismissing the thought. "It was my job."

"Job or not, you saved my life."

"I believe the more appropriate person for that designation is Agent Ivy."

Hearing his name made her heartache. In that painful, soul-shredding way. She swallowed her agony. "Well, he couldn't have done it without you. Or so I choose to believe."

"My informants tell me he left town."

She raised a brow at him. "What informants?"

The corner of his bushy mouth lifted. "My deputies. In fact, they told me they were pulled off your security detail just this morning."

Her throat turned dry. "True." According to the last officer outside her house, Jace Ivy had called and said they were no longer needed. Nice to know he was still in contact with *someone*. Just not her. She must not be as important to him. Something that grated along her heart as well as her pride.

"Does that mean big Mr. DEA agent solved his case?" he asked.

She shrugged. "I still haven't heard from him. Or Skye." The last detail of how he'd left her house practically sprinting for the hills after he learned something about "Slugger," she chose to keep quiet. She'd promised not to tell anyone. As damaged as her pride was, she wouldn't compromise his case. But at some point, the vast amount of evidence cluttering up her house had to be returned to the DEA. "Maybe that means whatever threat associated with the case is over. I'm relieved for your officers."

His smile turned sympathetic. "I'm sure you're relieved for yourself as well. That situation was most unfortunate. I shouldn't admit this, but my men enjoyed the work. We're a sleepy town out here, and it was a break from the norm."

"That's an understatement." She faked a chuckle. "Skye was always the one who wanted more thrilling adventures and dramatic flairs in life. Not me. This is too much for my tastes."

He collected the papers on the tray into a neat pile. "It's important for us to push ourselves a little out of our comfort zones every now and then. My wife says it's better for our hearts."

"Really? What would she say about near-death experiences?"

It was a long moment before he finally replied with a little strain behind his voice. "Those make everything after it that much brighter and more precious."

Her heart caved a little at that. Tears welled behind her eyes, and she struggled to hold them back. They'd both faced it together in different ways. He now had permanent scars to thank for it. She reached out and held his hand. He gripped back tightly, his own eyes a little glossy.

A loud alert sounded from the television, with the Breaking News banner a glaring red at the bottom of the screen. A man's picture was superimposed over live footage of some large compound in a rural area swarming with armed military personnel, covered in bullet-proof gear and blast shields. The man's face is what drew her attention.

Carlos Cabello. After all that research, she'd recognize that man anywhere.

The sheriff turned up the volume on the bed's attached remote.

"Mexican national and international drug lord Carlos Cabello was shot and killed this morning at his residence in northern Mexico in a coordinated raid with the Mexican

Army and the U.S. Drug Enforcement Agency. Witnesses claim the early morning incursion involved a heavy firefight that lasted more than an hour, with at least twenty conspirators dead on the compound. The cartel boss was indicted on over a dozen charges, including murder, drug trafficking, and money laundering. He had successfully eluded efforts to arrest him until a last-minute, highly confidential coordinated raid with U.S. law enforcement was carried out due to a recent tip on his whereabouts. No word as to what that tip was or from which agency. This culminates several cases against the Cabello cartel that had been ongoing for nearly a decade. The latest one involving the murder of a highly decorated DEA agent, Joseph Padilla, a year ago in El Paso, Texas."

A picture of Joe flashed on the screen in his official DEA uniform.

"Wow," she breathed. Before her eyes was the end of the mess in which she had been neck-deep over the last ten days.

Does this mean Skye and Reed can come home?

"I wonder if your Harley-riding agent was involved in that." The sheriff gave her a curious look.

She continued to watch, hoping for more information, or perhaps even a picture of Jace standing around in the aftermath. But the news helicopters didn't get close enough for face shots. For all she knew, he was down there in that chaos. Which would explain why he'd run out so quickly. Did he have to coordinate this? Though she doubted it. Something this big probably took much more than three days to arrange.

She made her goodbyes to Wyatt and promised to check in on him often.

When she made it home, four black sedans sat parked

outside her house. As she pulled into her driveway, more than a dozen agents piled out of the cars and met her at the door. Every one of them wore navy blue blazers with DEA emblazoned on the back, and had official gold badges dangling from chains around their necks.

Her heart leapt, thinking perhaps Jace was among them. Which meant he wasn't down in that dangerous fiasco in a Mexican drug compound. But with every face she saw, none of them were his.

"Miss Clark?"

She smiled politely, hiding her disappointment, and pulled her coat more tightly under her chin. "Are you here for Agent Ivy's evidence?"

"Yes. Thank you for your assistance. We'll collect everything so you can get back to your life."

She pressed her lips together and unlocked the door for them. Everything was still up on the walls and organized into various piles, just the way it was when Jace had left. She had no idea if he was going to return or not, and needed to continue where they left off. A small part of her heart hoped for that. Okay, fine, a large part of her heart.

"I didn't pack up anything yet. Would you like me to show you what I have and how it's organized?"

"No, thank you," the man replied. "We can take care of that."

All the agents brushed past her and started taking down all the photos and colored strings. Some of them a bit too quickly, and a few tacks flew off the corkboard. With robotic faces void of emotion and without any organization, they tossed the papers and files in open boxes.

She scowled, trying hard not to voice her displeasure at them dismantling all her hard work. "Um...coffee or tea?"

"No, thank you." He pointed to her kitchen table. "Is

this all the computer equipment Ivy confiscated?"

She nodded.

"Any thumb drives?"

"They're all in that box." She pointed to the one stacked on top of the chair.

In an amazingly fast time frame, they removed all the evidence from her home and stowed it in the multiple vehicles out front. The agents were thorough, systematic, and clinical in removing all traces of Jace Ivy. Her house looked barren—more Spartan-design—compared to the last few weeks.

"Miss Clark?" the agent called. "The paper with Monroe's passwords."

Her eyes widened. This man knew Reed? Or at least had clearly spoken to Jace. To make sure they captured everything they needed. Only Jace knew about that paper, aside from Reed himself. She went to the kitchen and pulled out the paper from the bottom of a junk drawer. "I tried to keep it safe."

He thanked her again without a smile and handed it to another collector, who put it on top of the last box, closing the lid.

"Last thing." He reached inside his suit pocket and pulled out a legal-sized envelope and handed it to her. "A reimbursement for your personal resources in assisting in this case, as well as the reward money for Emilio Cortez."

"Reward?" She glanced at the check. And nearly swallowed her tongue.

"Have a nice day." He turned and left, climbing into the lead sedan. All drove off in a dramatic procession.

Back inside, Lynée stared at the piece of paper, the words and numbers blurring together. The space felt so empty. So lonely. This was her home, the place she was the happiest, aside from the library, but she couldn't contain the grief consuming her insides.

He didn't even bother to come back himself. To gather the evidence they had worked so hard to decipher, had poured over together side-by-side. Had risked both their lives over. Because he didn't love her. Because he didn't want to lift her hopes that they had a chance together. There was no chance. He was only here for the case. She was just a fun time in the sack, an entertaining side-job.

That kiss outside her house was a goodbye kiss.

Somehow, this was worse than Todd leaving her. With him, it was just bruised pride. This time she actually had a piece of her soul missing.

With two hands on the paper, she nearly ripped the check in half. She stopped herself and let out an audible sigh. Lord, how she wanted to. She didn't want his money. She wanted him. That didn't seem to work into his plans.

"Keep it, Lynnie. The church could use this." She glanced down through blurry vision. Sure, maybe something good could come out of a broken heart.

CHAPTER 31

JACE HAD TIMED this operation at precisely the same moment as the Cabello raid. He and five other DEA agents merged from various doors on the sixth floor of DEA Headquarters in Springfield, Virginia. They didn't want to alert anyone to the upcoming arrest and give the target a chance to escape.

Three days before, he'd raced from Lynée's house straight to the airport to take the first flight back to his office in Detroit. He even left his beloved bike sitting in a garage at SeaTac. There was far too much for him to track down based on the newest evidence. He hadn't even had the time to call Lynée and tell her what was going on.

Or he should say he hadn't *made* the time. He was far too angry to make that call.

Several people poked their heads over the cubicle walls, watching the intimidating group march down the final hallway. The other agents stayed just outside the last office door and let Jace enter on his own, as planned.

Phil sat at his expansive desk, looking at his computer screen. From his shitty shave job and dark circles under his eyes, he clearly hadn't slept much. Several opened cans of diet soda sat off to the side. The tall window behind him displayed a decent view of the dark gray Potomac River snaking by the building.

Jace tightened his grip on the file in his hand and knocked on the open door.

His mentor looked over and grinned. Then he instantly lost his smile the second he saw Jace's scowl. "Jace? What's wrong?" He stood but didn't move around the desk.

"You set me up."

"What happened?" The blindsided look Phil gave looked genuine.

He'd never realized how great of an actor his mentor really was. Jace took one step forward. "You let them send me out there to cover up your dirty work. So you could keep your cushy little perch here at your desk. To pin your dirty shit on another agent. What's worse, you led that assassin right to me. You betrayed me."

For a split second, recognition dawned in Phil's eyes. In half a blink, he switched from figuring out how Jace found out to figuring out how he could save himself. He recovered quickly. Had anyone else approached him with this accusation, he probably would've succeeded at convincing them. "I have no idea what happened out there or what you heard. But son, listen to me. I would never—"

"I'm not your son." He slammed the file on the desk. "I'm not your *slugger* anymore, either."

The facade slipped a little, a small line of sweat appearing at his balding hairline. He grabbed the file and looked at the first page.

A copy of Joe Padilla's report.

"Does that look familiar?" Jace asked. "You're the only other person who ever saw it. You are on a very short list of people who have the access to make an official report disappear from the system. You made sure any file that could potentially reveal your alias was removed. The same fucking nickname you used with me in Little League. You sick son of a bitch."

His face paled. "This is not what you think it was."

"That report only got me started. It didn't take me long to connect all the off-shore accounts the cartel sent payments to over the last fifteen years...*your* accounts."

"That has to be a mistake, Jace. I would never—"

"I should've known." He moved another step, to corner him behind the desk. "When you bought that boat. And that luxury Mercedes for your wife. Was my college tuition paid for by Cabello payoffs too, Phil? Do you remember the look on my mother's face when you gave me that check? The relief...her tears of grief that my father wasn't there to see it."

Phil tossed the file back on his desk, his expression turning dismissive with a tinge of anger behind it. Damn, he must've practiced this moment. "Back off, Ivy. All the intel you have is wrong. These are planted. To throw us off the scent of the real mole."

He shook his head, forcing himself to control his breathing. It was the only way he could get out of this room without strangling this bastard to death. "Then you actually had the audacity to ask where I'd hidden Monroe. Only *hours* after we released the picture of the cartel assassin, Emilio Cortez. Cabello called you, didn't he? Threatening you to find Monroe. I was too blind to see it. To even consider the possibility. But it was you. *You* are responsible for the death of two seasoned agents, and framing a third."

His gaze turned cold. "Two?"

Gotcha. "Joe Padilla." He stepped closer. They were only a foot apart.

Phil didn't step back. Just lifted his chin. Daring Jace to punch it.

"And my father." Jace growled the last few words.

Finally, the actor broke. Into a cold, calculating man he barely recognized. "You have no idea what we faced. Other agents caught, tortured to death, and their families threatened. I didn't have a choice. I chose to save your life."

"You chose to save your own."

"They were going to kill my wife, and you and your mother. If I didn't start helping them. They knew where you lived. They had your picture, Jace. You were only eleven years old."

"So, you gave up my father—your own fucking partner—to save your ass." He closed the distance, and Phil actually stepped back. "Fifteen years later, you give *me* up. Cabello threatens you because the DEA is getting too close to him again, and you hand Padilla and Monroe over on a platter. Only Monroe escaped. Pissing off the cartel more. You scramble to save your ass and use me to find him for you."

Jace lunged forward, grabbed Phil's shoulders, and threw him against the window. His mentor fought back, trying to shake him off. But the man was out of shape and not nearly as full of rage as Jace. He yanked the man's arms behind him, keeping his face pinned against the glass. After the handcuffs were secure and Jace removed Phil's service pistol from the holster at his hip, he leaned forward and muttered in the man's ear. "And you were going to let them kill me."

"You were the one who put Monroe in hiding," he groaned. "You should have just brought him in. You left me no choice. They were going to kill me if I didn't turn you over. I had to give them someone."

"Yeah. Anyone but you." He yanked Phil off the window and shoved him hard into the arms of the waiting agents who entered at the sound of a struggle. Two of them seized Phil's computer and the files on his desk.

They made the man stand there as they ripped through his entire office. What Phil didn't know was a whole other team was ransacking his home right then.

"Don't do this, Jace. I helped you make something of your life. After your father died, I stepped in. I took care of you and your mother. I gave you your college degree. I made you a DEA agent. You owe your whole damn life to me."

His knuckles whitened, the urge to knock this guy out so damn strong. "You *took* my life from me when you murdered my father. Fuck you, Phil."

The agents holding him moved him toward the door, pulling him backward by the cuffs.

"No, wait!" the old man yelled.

They stopped.

The bastard's face changed again, this time to a defeated, desperate plea. Almost like he was about to cry. "You might as well just kill me now. Cabello will find a way to get to me in prison."

"You have no idea how tempted I am to do that." His voice shook with rage. He decided not to let his former mentor know the Cabello compound was being raided. The man deserved to sweat in terror for a while.

Finally, Phil was dragged from the room.

Jace watched the steel waters of the Potomac swirl by the window. Not nearly as turbulent as the storm raging inside him. The flight from Seattle had been full of this frenzy, a rampage against those he'd trusted.

Lynée had been included in that mental rampage. An irrational feeling, since none of this was her fault. But she'd been the one to uncover the connection to his surrogate father. To the one who'd looked after him and pulled him off the troubled path in his youth. If she hadn't found that file, Phil would still be his mentor. His life not upturned, his career not over, and his reputation not forever tarnished.

"You can't trust anyone," he muttered. As if the river could actually hear him. If Phil fooled him this well for this long, Lynée could fool him just as easily. He was right to keep people at a distance. It was the only way to make sure he'd never be duped again.

"She's better off without me."

Suddenly, the conversation they shared about power flooded his mind. How real power was in mercy and forgiveness. But at this moment, in this fucked-up situation of betrayal and duplicity, mercy was a weakness. Mercy was something scumbags like Cabello and Phil used to exploit to their own advantage. To use their boot heels to keep others down, while they were soaking themselves in their forgiveness desperate to regain power. Which was hopeless. How much power did those sorry suckers have when they offered mercy?

Jace leaned his forehead against the cool glass. When had his face gotten so damn hot? This world was unforgiving. Full of disappointment and desperation. He was doing Lynée a favor by keeping her as far from this twisted reality as possible. She deserved her life full of mercy. Happiness. Innocence.

That's how she would always remain in his mind. Innocent. The epitome of what was good in the world. A good that was rare and had to be protected. And free from being tainted. Tainted by his own inability to see mercy as power.

CHAPTER 32

Two days later

SKYE AND REED sat across from Lynée at the dining room table. Her best friend had cooked an amazing Thanksgiving meal for the three of them, to celebrate their return home. The lovebirds were all cuddly and cozy beside each other, filling each other's plates with food. They'd spent so much time alone together while in hiding, and Skye had clearly loved it. But she loved being home more, that much was obvious. In her own home, with Reed.

Lynée might have been tempted to throw up at their displays of affection. But in all honesty, it made her heart crack.

How much she'd wanted that with Jace...

Two days before and only a few hours after the Cabello compound was raided and the cartel boss killed, Skye and Reed had been escorted down from the lake cabin back home by a DEA agent, not Jace. Their protective custody was over. The threat was neutralized. Along with an official letter from headquarters, Reed Monroe was no longer a suspect in the murder of his partner, Joe Padilla, and his arrest warrant rescinded. His superiors requested his return to the El Paso office for a final debrief before reinstatement.

After Thanksgiving.

Reed had already promised Skye he would submit his resignation the second he walked in that office.

"You still haven't heard from him?" Skye asked her, with a face like an injured kitten.

Lynée shook her head and finished off her glass of white wine. Her appetite had been next to non-existent since the day Jace had left. But there was no way she was missing this monumental moment with Skye. Her return home. She'd missed her so much.

"The amount of paperwork he's buried under right now might take weeks for him to sort through." Reed refilled her glass without asking. "That kind of operation against the cartel is no small feat. The red tape is insane. Give him some time."

She smiled back, a small fake one. His attempts at trying to make her feel better weren't working. Mainly because she knew better. But that was the kind of guy Reed was. Kind, thoughtful, and hated seeing others in pain. He was perfect for Skye. The flame between them would burn brightly for years to come, she was sure of it.

"So," Lynée cleared her throat. "Is Reed Monroe going to return to the diner as a short-order cook? Or do we still need to call you Guy Hancock?"

The lovebirds shared an adoring look.

"I think Guy Hancock is gone," he replied. "But Ralph will have to find a different chef."

Skye held his hand on the table cloth. "Reed's going to open his own cybersecurity consulting firm."

Lynée smiled, a real one this time. "Wow. Are you allowed to touch electronics now?"

He laughed.

"I'm happy for you. Let me know when you're ready.

I'd love to invest in your startup."

"I appreciate that, Lynée. I'm very honored by your faith in me. But I have some money saved I'd like to use."

She shrugged, lifted her glass in another toast. "To a new beginning."

They raised their own wines and drank to that.

With the delicious meal over and the dishes cleared, Reed offered to clean up in the kitchen. Giving the two best friends a chance to chat in private in the living room.

Skye's house had been cleaned up only a few days after the break-in, and the locks changed. The back door still had a plywood cover over the window but was scheduled to be replaced next week. Skye still insisted on having Thanksgiving dinner at her house. Which Lynée welcomed. Her own house reminded her too much of Jace. Of their amazing love sessions and their hours of research. Everywhere she looked was a reminder of him. She did everything she could to stay out of her own home, going back only to shower and sleep.

"What's your next step?" Skye asked, curling up on the sofa. A cozy fire flickered and crackled in the fireplace. A light snowfall fell outside the window behind her head. Winter had arrived in more ways than one.

She wiped a piece of fuzz off the sofa cushion. Mainly just to keep her hands busy. "When I'm not at work, I've been helping the church with their upcoming children's Christmas play. Several of the costumes needed repair, and I'm making a new set of wings for Archangel Gabriel, who managed to allow his dog to get a hold of the last pair."

"It's in three weeks?"

"Ten days."

"I'd love to be there. Let me know if you need help."

She nodded and stared into the fire.

"You've been wearing more makeup," her friend announced.

"Just eyeliner and mascara."

Skye's smile widened. "And you're wearing the blouse I gave you for your birthday last year. Not one of those oversized sweaters you love so much."

"It's Thanksgiving. Aren't we supposed to dress up a little?"

"Not just today. The day we came home, too. You were in a push-up bra and form-fitting tunic. He really did have an effect on you."

Lynée lost her smile. Yeah, *he* really did. In so many ways.

"Does this mean you're willing to consider dating again?"

"No." She rubbed her eyebrow, needing the pressure to distract her. To keep her eyes from welling with tears. The very idea of dating other guys right now made her want to crawl under a rock in the woods.

"What if Jace returned? Would you—"

"He's not coming back," she cut her off. "Please, can we just drop it?"

Skye bit her lip and set her glass on the coffee table. She scooted closer to her friend on the couch. "Don't shut yourself off, Lynnie. And don't give up. You were the one who told me to fight for what I loved."

"I did. I fought to bring you home. All that time you were in hiding, I never stopped looking through all Reed's evidence. So you could come home. Because I love you."

"I know you do. And I can never thank you enough for that. Jace said you were incredible, and he'd never seen someone so dedicated and determined. All your timelines and strings and photos connecting everything

215

together...you're the one who solved this. You're the one who brought us home."

Lynée stared at her friend, stunned. "You talked to him?"

Skye's lips parted. "Shit. I'm sorry. I wasn't supposed to say anything."

"What the hell?" Lynée muttered. "When?"

She gasped. "Lynnie, you cursed."

"When did you talk to him, Skye?!"

She sighed and cast Reed a sideways glance when he entered the living room. "The day before we came back. Told us everything would be over in twenty-four hours, and we needed to be ready to go the next morning."

"He called *you?*" It was impossible to keep her voice down. "Why wouldn't he call me? He didn't think I deserved the courtesy of an update? With *his* evidence all over *my* house?"

"I have no idea, Lynnie. At the time, he said we weren't allowed to contact anyone yet." Skye tried to calm down her friend, but she was way too fired up to allow that.

"After everything I'd been through...*we'd* been through, to help solve *his* case... After all those nights, those *amazing nights* and sweet nothings were just that to him...nothing." Tears pricked her eyes. "He just runs out the front door without a damn word, and he calls you."

Skye's cheeks turned pink. "He didn't give us any details. He raved about how hard you worked. I could hear it in his voice, Lynée. He's nuts about you."

Anger and agony fused together in her brain, and she just couldn't take it anymore. She shook the tears from her eyes, only to have more replace them. "I have to go." She stood and raced to grab her coat and purse.

"Please, don't leave like this," Skye urged. "You need to

calm down before you get behind the wheel."

Reed stepped toward the door—maybe to block her way or maybe just to open it for her—his face full of concern.

"No!" she fumbled with putting on her coat. "I should've known better. He was only here for the case, and the second we solved it, he was literally kicking up dust under his boots as he ran off." Tears spilled out of her eyes, and she brushed them angrily away, fighting with her zipper. "There is no such thing as chivalry. There is no such thing as true love. It's all fake!" She yanked on the clasp, and it ripped off. "Ugh! I *hate* this stupid coat!" Tears streamed down her cheeks.

"We'll get you a new one," Skye urged, and grabbed for her own. "Let me drive you home. Please, sweetie. And more importantly, you know true love is real. You're surrounded by it every day. In all those books, those biographies, documentaries...there's a whole section for romance."

The words snapped her out of despair and fully into the realm of disgust. "This is not a damn romance novel, Skye Winters, no matter how many you read. This is real life. Tragedies and disappointments."

She whirled and reached for the door.

Reed stood in front of it, determined not to let her pass.

"Move aside, Reed Monroe, or so help me God, I will bash you across the head with my purse."

With sunken shoulders, he opened the door and let her go.

CHAPTER 33

LYNÉE LEANED OVER a child, maybe five or six, fixing the angel's wings, so they flared out more. She smiled and gave the boy some encouraging words.

From the shadows in the back of the church, Jace witnessed the simple interaction. His heart swelled with so much tenderness, he could have fallen over with a single breath of frigid wind from outside.

After essentially decimating the Cabello Cartel and shackling Phil in cuffs, Jace should be happy. Proud and accomplished. A career-catapulting bust. Instead, a gaping-damn-hole was left where his heart barely beat.

There was only one thing that could fill that hole. The gorgeous strawberry-blonde in a red Christmas sweater with fake elf legs dangling from the front. When he'd gone to her house to find it empty, and done the same at Skye's home, he knew his last two choices were either the library or the church.

Jace's attention snapped when the audience applauded. Kids rushed from the stage to behind the curtains, some grabbing props that threatened to accidentally knock other children in the head. It was pure chaos. But in the midst of all that, he could feel nothing but love. Which scared the shit out of him.

There was no way she'd take him back. Not after what had happened.

The way he'd left Lynée was an asshole move. He could see that now. Even his mother had scolded him at Thanksgiving. He'd just up and left without a single word, his mind too focused on his rage and what steps he had to take to protect the evidence. To coordinate a joint raid with Mexican officials. Then he'd felt too damn guilty to call her and explain.

He'd vacillated for several days, each moment the truth of what he needed to do staring at him hard. He'd forgotten that in his world of disappointments and desperation, there had to be light to keep him from giving into despair. Innocence was what he needed. Crusaders fought for what was good and just. That was where real power came from. Lynée was his power. The living embodiment of what he fought for.

A plastic roll-cart bumped him from the side.

"Goodness, sorry," Wanda called from beside him. "I can't steer this thing worth a darn." The older woman looked frazzled.

"No problem. Why don't I help?"

"Oh, Jace." Her eyes widened. "I didn't recognize you without your beard."

He rubbed his chin, the skin feeling like a hairless kitten. He hadn't felt his bare jaw in years. He turned his attention to Lynée.

In a flash, her head lifted and met his gaze. Her eyebrows lifted, and a touch of pink graced her cheeks.

"This is for the final act," Wanda stole his attention. "If you could just wheel it over there." She pointed to the side wall, and as Jace pushed the cart, he could feel Lynée's eyes on him.

"Perfect." Wanda went to help the next little one with her costume.

Jace approached the woman he loved slowly, abundantly aware of how quickly this could blow up in his face. "Hi."

"Hi," Lynée began softly. Then her words took on a stronger edge. "How long were you standing there?"

"Miss Lynée, my crown is bent." A young boy cut in, holding his plastic crown, his eyes filling with tears.

She took the crown and adjusted it. "No problem, Jason, look. All fixed."

He smiled as she put it back on his head.

More people came into the large room and filled the seats. The murmurs escalated, along with his heart rate.

She grabbed Jace's hand and moved them away from the congestion. "How long have you been here?" She stared him down.

Coming from a five-foot-five fireball, he was scared. Actually terrified.

Oh shit. "Just a few minutes." He swallowed hard. He couldn't do this here. "Is there someplace we can talk?"

"No. I'm in the middle of something if you can't tell." She stretched her arm out before crossing them in front of her.

Wanda stepped over to them. "Lynée, if you need to leave, you can. Sally and I have everything under control. They're on the final act, and I have no doubt I can get the parents to help clean up." She nodded and sent an earnest look their way.

"Please," Jace implored. He had one chance to get this right.

She sighed, her chest falling on the exhale. "Fine. Let's—" her eyes scanned the space. Kids ran everywhere, getting ready for the final act of the play. "Let's go outside."

He followed her toward the door. She retrieved her coat from the hooks off to the side, and he helped her slip it on. Then he held the door open for her. The crisp, cold air nearly burned his freshly-shaven skin. A beard was an advantage in this frigid air. Mother Nature decidedly not making it easy for him.

They moved down the brick steps off to the side by the stone benches. Light snow flurries floated down around them, melting once they reached the pavement.

"I didn't think I'd see you again." She looked up at him, again, arms crossed, clutching her coat tight against her.

"I know. I'm sorry about the way I left, and I'm sorry...I'm sorry I couldn't tell you why I left."

Her perfect eyebrows pulled together.

He exhaled. "The report you read...Slugger...I knew who that was."

"You know who the mole is?"

He nodded. "It was Phil."

She gasped. "Phil?" She reached a hand, touching his forearm. "Oh, no. I'm so sorry."

He reached a hand clasping her arm in return, longing for that connection to never break again. "I'm the one who should be sorry." He shook his head. "Lynée, you came into my life and turned it upside down. You were the last thing I expected." He stepped closer and placed a second hand on her arm. "I was scared because, well, I felt more myself than ever. Shit, I'm not making any sense." He ran a hand over his raw chin. Damn, it felt so weird.

She kept her eyes on him, patiently waiting.

He hadn't rehearsed what he was going to say; he just knew he had to convince her. "Most of my life, maybe all of my life, I felt I wasn't good enough. That I always had to prove myself." He shrugged a shoulder. "In my job, my superiors thought I was driven, and I only became more successful. But ultimately, the fear still lingered. Somehow, being with you, the fear fades. Maybe that's another reason I ran."

"Is that why you always seem so intense?"

He snorted. "Probably." He closed the gap, cupping his hands around Lynée's beautiful face. "I'm sorry I ran. It won't happen again. Please... forgive me." He smoothed a thumb over her plump Tinkerbell lips. "Do you think you can find it in your heart to show mercy on me? To forgive me. And to take me back?"

She stared up at him with watery eyes. "Yes," she breathed.

Sweet Jesus! He leaned down to kiss his Bell, feeling like it was the first time. He prayed he'd get to do this every day for the rest of his life. Their tongues danced together, warming him to his core.

"Bell," he breathed over her lips.

Her cold hands cupped his face. "You shaved off your beard."

He closed his eyes and savored her soft skin on his. "I did it for you. Thought you'd like it better."

Her eyes twinkled up at him. "I was getting used to the beard."

"I'll grow it back, then."

She chuckled. "No rush." Her arms slipped inside his leather jacket and wrapped around his waist.

"Please let me take you home."

She looked back at the church, then at him. "Okay. Let me text Skye."

He waited as patiently as he could. But this new feeling of relief paired with a tinge of fear, even still. Fear that she would change her mind and want to take it back. When she was done, she smiled and took his hand. The fear disappeared.

He led her to his bike in the full parking lot. He popped the seat open and pulled out her pink helmet.

Without hesitation, she let him strap it on her head. They settled on his bike, and the sensation of her arms around him warmed him from the outside in. Amazing how she had control over his feelings. With her, he wasn't afraid.

The flurries increased, with bright puffy snowflakes falling faster. They all melted as they hit the road, but a light coat covered the grassy areas like a thin frosting.

In the brief minutes it took to get to her house, his nerves climbed to new heights. So anxious to show her how much he loved her.

The second he lifted the helmet off, he claimed her mouth again. He ached for this woman on so many levels.

No sense delaying it. "Lynée, I'm not a flowery guy."

She chuckled. "I know that."

Her eyes sparkling at him gave him a confidence boost.

"What I do know is that I love you. I want you in my life." He pulled the ring from his jeans pocket. "Would you wear this for the rest of your life?"

Her precious jaw dropped, not something he'd seen very often with his Bell. "Yes," she choked out, a tear streaming down her cheek.

He slid it on her finger and kissed her madly. The neighbors may be watching, but they better get used to it. He'd give her thousands more of these no matter who was watching. He led her inside. Strangely, walking through that door and into that room felt like home. Now he only had one thing on his mind.

He took her hand, freezing from the motorcycle ride

through the snow. He cupped her dainty fingers in his palms, and breathed into them, warming them up.

"Jace, I love you." Her voice was breathy like she'd been holding in the words and too afraid to speak them aloud. He knew that feeling. He wanted to make sure she never felt afraid around him, ever.

He raised his gaze to hers, her smiling face so beautiful it stole his breath.

"I love you, too."

He slipped off her coat then his jacket. Hands roaming her body, he, not-so-discreetly, started working on shedding their clothes.

She lifted her eyebrows.

"Bell, I can't wait another minute."

Her pants hit the floor. She jumped into his arms and crushed her lips to his.

His dick pressed against her center, causing her to moan. One of the most beautiful sounds to his ears. He spun her to the closest wall, working on his jeans.

Gingerly, he slipped a finger under her panties, testing her. She was already wet and swollen.

"Jace," she begged.

"Bell, what do you think if I don't use protection?" He freed his cock from his garments.

She stared at him. "Really?"

"Your call, sweetheart. You want babies. You'd be a brilliant mother. I'd love to give you babies. As many as you want."

Tears flooded her eyes again. "Yes. I say, yes. Make love to me, Jace."

He kissed her fiercely, then moved to her cheeks to kiss away her tears.

Keeping her gaze, he pulled her panties down and

slowly pushed inside. Her channel was so slick, so hot. Without the protective layer of a condom, the sensations wrapped around his dick heightened the pleasure. He had to grit his teeth to keep from coming right then. "I can't wait to see your belly swollen with my baby. Bell, I want to give you the world."

Her eyes fluttered closed as he pulled back and pushed in deeper. As he picked up speed, her precious mouth formed an O, and she panted the closer she came to her orgasm.

"How does that feel?" he rasped. *Please let it feel as insanely incredible to you as it does for me.*

"So warm," she panted. "So sensitive, I don't know if I can..."

"You can, sweetheart. You're so beautiful. I love you, Lynée."

"Ah, Jace. I love you."

With just a few more thrusts, she cried out, her eyes closed and her cheeks flushed. Her sweet channel squeezed around his cock, milking him over and over until he couldn't hold back.

He released inside her, giving over every ounce of power left in him. This incredible woman was now his; he was now hers, in every way. They belonged to each other. For eternity.

He held her tight against the wall, catching his breath, before sliding them down to the carpeted floor of her living room. This was just the beginning. They had years and years of more escapades against doors, kitchen counters, on sofas, and in the bedroom. He could hardly wait.

He wrapped her in his arms. Their gazes locked; nothing needed to be said. The moment was perfect.

Lynée spoke softly. "So, are you moving in here?"

"Yes, unless you want another house."

"When do you want to get married?"

"Immediately."

She lifted her eyebrows. "Okay," and grinned. "What about your job?"

"I resigned."

She sighed. "What will you do?"

"I don't know." He couldn't help but grin at her millions of questions. She *would* make a good agent.

"The sheriff is retiring. Could use an experienced man with plenty of talent to replace him."

That sounded like something Jace would enjoy. Definitely a break from the grind of the DEA. Plus, he could be home with his new family every night. That would be the best thing in the world.

He rose and slipped off her glasses, resting them on the coffee table. Then he lifted his fiancée over his shoulder and made his way to the stairs.

"Jace! Put me down." She swatted his ass.

"Not gonna happen, Bell. I have some lost time to make up for in pleasuring you." Time that would start now and take decades to finish.

The End

A MESSAGE FROM THE AUTHORS

Thank you so much for reading Renegade!

If you enjoyed this story, please consider posting a review at one or more of your favorite retailers, as well as Goodreads. Even a short review, one or two lines, can be a tremendous help and encouragement to the authors. Your review is also a gift to other readers who may be searching for just this sort of story, and will be grateful you helped them find it.

Thank you!

Mia London & Susan Sheehey

OTHER NOVELS

Other Novels By Susan Sheehey

Sweet Escape Series
Dry Spell
Hot Spell
Cold Spell

Royals of Solana Series Boxset
Prince of Solana
Jewel of Solana
Crown of Solana
Royal Wedding novella

Knights of Texas Series
Tell Me What You Want
Tell Me What You Crave
Tell Me What You Need
Tell Me What You Feel

Audrey's Promise

Summer Heat: Imperfectly Yours Anthology

ABOUT THE AUTHORS

Mia London

Mia London loves to write.

After reading fiction for years, she decided it was finally time to put those images and scenes floating around in her head down on paper.

She is a huge fan of romance, highly optimistic, and wildly faithful to the HEA (happily ever after). Her goal is to create a fantasy you will enjoy with characters you could love.

She lives in Texas with her attentive, loving, supermodel husband, and perfectly behaved, brilliant children. Her produce never wilts, there are no weeds in her flowerbeds, and chocolate is her favorite food group.

http://www.facebook.com/MiaLondonAuthor
http://www.twitter.com/MiaLondonAuthor
http://www.goodreads.com/author/show/8414916.Mia_London
MiaLondon.com
Email: mia@mialondon.com

Susan Sheehey

Susan Sheehey writes contemporary romance and romantic suspense adventure. Water plays a crucial element in all her novels, and she's a strong advocate for autism awareness and acceptance. She squeezes in writing time between chauffeuring around her two boys and guzzling down French vanilla coffee. Her beloved husband keeps her relatively sane and full of laughter. She and her family live in Texas.

SusanSheehey.com
http://www.facebook.com/SusanSheehey
http://www.twitter.com/SusieQWriter
http://www.bookbub.com/authors/susan-sheehey
http://www.goodreads.com/author/show/7189847.Susan _Sheehey

Join her newsletter for monthly announcements, updates, and special giveaways here:
https://landing.mailerlite.com/webforms/landing/p5b0i9

Interested in Advance Reader Copies of Susan's upcoming novels?
Let her know here:
https://www.SusanSheehey.com/Contact